Owned

Darkly Ever Afterverse
Book 1

L.V. Lane

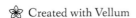 Created with Vellum

Contents

Chapter One

Ava

Stuck between the inner and outer door was a lonely place to be. My lips tightened as I glanced at the Colt in my hand before tucking it into the deep pocket of my coat. It was old and had a tendency to jam, which meant I had a fifty-fifty chance that it would be of any use. That said, I had no desire to be in a situation where I needed to use it. If it came down to killing, or even wounding someone, I prayed that my self-preservation instinct kicked in. Etiquette had no place in the post-apocalyptic world.

Still, how a person handled fear was not something you knew, not until you were called upon to face it, and by then, it was far too late.

The one-minute warning flashed up on the door panel, and my adrenaline kicked in. I wasn't supposed to be out here, and the wrongness was like an oversized raincoat that no amount of belt-tightening could make fit.

"Are you sure you're okay with this, Ava?" Nora had asked, her frown one of concern. I blinked, driving the memory away. We needed medical supplies. Unfortunately, our small combat-trained team had been cut off, leaving the community in an unusual situation of needing to fend for itself. Their message had been garbled due to interference, but it was clear something had kicked off. It happened from time to time—the changing ownership of the surrounding districts was nothing new. The fact remained that our team would not be returning for several days, possibly weeks.

I was the best of the remaining residents, which wasn't saying much.

My past life—the life I had been born to—was long gone. My parents were wealthy, and my life a coveted one. They had aspirations for me; I had plenty myself. That once joyous future had died along with them.

The harsh reality of anarchy was that it cared little for who you once were. The good, the bad, the rich, and the poor held no context in the bounds of chaos. I had watched mothers fight over food in those dark days immediately after the collapse. They might have been friends once in that other world, but not anymore. The need to survive ripped everything else away; considerations, respect, compassion even. They held no sway when your baby was so hungry it had barely the energy to cry.

Things were better now—a little.

The ten-second count sent a spike to my heart rate. I fluctuated between a firm belief that I could do this and a terrible fear I couldn't until the hiss of the outer door opening dropped the entire self-discussion because it was all now very pointless.

A strange calm replaced the panic. It was dark, and the air felt sharp and cold against my face. It had been so long since I'd felt air on my face, real air, not the processed, filtered stuff inside, that I was cast back to the garden of my childhood home. The memory was so vivid that I could almost feel the springy grass beneath my bare toes, and smell the sweet scent of the honeysuckle that grew over the stone walls.

The stench of diesel drifted on the air, thrusting me back to the present with an unpleasant jolt.

I stepped outside and turned to watch the outer-door close behind me, sealing access. Separation became a crushing weight. I was here now, on the streets, and I would not be going back until I had gotten what was needed.

A deep breath helped as I surveyed the immediate area. It was wet, and although it wasn't raining, the air held moisture like it could turn at any moment. Deserted; the surveillance before leaving had indicated this, but it could change, and like the weather, it could change at any time.

I knew the route by memory, and with a final lingering glance at that sealed door, I headed off.

Nora

"I'm worried about Ava," I said. I was talking to Mary, but my focus was all on my baby boy. Civilization had imploded, but the tiny, needy bundle in my arms only instilled the keenest sense of wonder. My love for him was absolute.

Enough to let my friend leave to get the medication he needed.

The thought of Ava coming to harm terrified me, but not nearly as much as the thought of losing my son. I'd wanted to go, but the birth had been complicated, and nine months later, I was still struggling to regain my strength.

With a surname like O'Reilly and red hair, it was fair to say there was a bit of Irish blood in me. Once upon a time, I'd had the temper to match and considered myself mentally tough.

Life had gotten complicated long before Adam; it was a thousand times worse now. But I only had to look at his innocent face to know what was important. If my emotions sometimes got the better of me now, I would get over it for Adam's sake.

"She'll be fine," Mary said. "Whatever's happening in the northern district appears to be isolated. Added bonus of keeping things quiet around here."

Despite being in her seventies, Mary was still sprightly and resilient as hell. People rarely talked about the world before—too painful—so I didn't know her story. But I got the impression Mary was a survivor of more than the societal collapse. She volunteered to go in Ava's place since she could handle a gun and herself, even at seventy-something. Ava wasn't biting, and this, despite me believing that Mary had the edge if it went to the wire.

Mary leaned over the console to take the monitoring keys and manually rotated through the surveillance cameras. The operation room was empty except for the two of us. From here, we could monitor all the outside camera feeds. Not that we were expecting Ava back yet, but there was comfort in watching the screens and seeing that everything remained quiet.

The data center that became a home to our community consisted of nearly thirty people. Somewhere along the line, it had been named Sanctuary. In the seventeen years since the war had ended, a lot had changed in society, if you could even call it society any more. I'd lived more years in the afterlife, and memories of that old world held only a dream-like quality in my mind. I'd moved around a lot before finding Sanctuary. Disparity existed between the many pockets of humanity. Each had their culture, rules, and laws, or lack thereof.

I had lived in communities of thousands and of five. They'd all had a common theme. I'd run from one to another, always hoping for better until the day I crossed paths with Sanctuary scouts. It had sounded too good to be true. But I was pregnant, alone, and desperate enough to take a risk. As it turned out, it was the best risk I'd ever taken and the start of something good.

"She knows where to go and what to do," Mary said, reminding me that while Sanctuary was good, the world at large was not. "And she cares about Adam as much as you. She won't take risks in this, not where her favorite little boy is concerned."

I smiled, but it faded. "Yeah, it's more her killer instinct that worries me."

Mary made a scoffing noise and the corners of her eyes crinkled in amusement. "She doesn't belong on this side of the apocalypse, that's for sure. But I don't reckon any of us do. Maybe except my Walt. I'd have liked to see that bastard suffer some, but he went and had a heart attack the day before the shit hit the fan. Some folks have all the luck."

"How come I'm only hearing about your nefarious plans for this mysterious Walt now?" I teased.

She cackled to herself before wiping tears of laughter from her eyes.

Her humor faded, and she huffed out a sigh. "Ah, Nora, don't you feel it?" She gestured toward the monitors where the damp, dark streets remained eerily quiet. "Change is coming. Don't know if it's a good kind of change, like the day I happened upon Sanctuary. Or the bad kind, like the day I happened on my Walt. But it's coming, and not a damn thing either of us can do about it. We can only buckle up and get ready for the ride. Don't talk about the past much. That's the rule. Don't think of it much either, truth be told. Except for times like these when the hustling begins again."

Her words settled a heaviness on my shoulders and a sickness in my gut.

Jodi and our reconnaissance team had been cut off by the distant troubles in the northern district. Now, Ava was on the streets, and Ava never went out. Jodi handled that side of things.

Jodi was tough as fucking nails so Ava didn't need to be.

The history between those two had happened after the collapse, but I still didn't know much about it. There was speculation—there was always speculation within a community, but especially one with only thirty people. Jodi had decked a newly arrived soldier when he'd tried it on with Ava. It was fair to say she was protective. Heck, they slept in the same bed. It didn't take a rocket scientist to work out that they were together in a way that went beyond friends.

We all had a history. Things we recalled fondly and things we'd like to forget.

It was clear the two women came from different sides of the track prior to the collapse. Afterward, new lines had formed, and it was survival of the fittest. The rest of us were just hanging on for as long as we could. My mind stretched into wondering what we would do if the team never returned.

Mary leaned across and patted my hand, her gnarly knuckles scraped tight against skin made fragile with age. "She'll be fine. Nine out of ten times, they never see a soul during an op."

"It's the one in ten that worries me," I said. As I locked gazes with Mary, I noticed the tightness in her face. "If someone gets hold of her—"

"They won't," Mary pushed back firmly.

The urge to cry rose. Adam slept on, oblivious to the

turmoil his small presence wrecked upon our tiny part of the world.

Like a creeping tide, fear could never be banished completely in the post-apocalyptic world.

I knew if anyone should catch Ava, I would never see my friend again.

Chapter Two

Ava

Three days had passed since I'd left Sanctuary, during which the conflict in the northern district had both escalated and expanded.

Rain pelted the rooftop where I had hunkered down to hide. It was midday, and grey clouds rolled relentlessly overhead. The distant roar of combat, the put-put of weapons firing and the occasional boom of a louder discharge, blended into the hopeless cacophony of war.

It had been years since I'd been outside. Jodi had been with me last time, a comforting and protective presence that had made it tolerable.

I should have been back by now, but the largest battle I'd seen in a decade had thwarted those plans. I wondered if Jodi and the team were trapped outside, their fate as precarious as mine. Should any of us be captured, Sanctuary would be compromised, and that meant the lives of everyone inside. The former data center-turned-home was right in the middle of these two warring factions. The conflict had ignored it so far. We'd seen such troubles before. They had always passed us by, but something about this time roused a sense of *inevitability*.

Given the scale of activity and my questionable skills, I couldn't see myself avoiding detection much longer. Yesterday, I'd attempted to return, but the streets had been crawling with soldiers brandishing enough firepower to render my temperamental Colt useless. The endless scenarios of being discovered haunted me. In most of them, my assailant had laughed when the stupid gun had jammed.

I thought I ought to feel more rage, but three days without food had taken its toll, and all my emotions remained muted. Finding water had been easy enough given the weather. My immune system had been genetically modified long before the collapse and handled the dirty source. The lack of food had bothered me at first. Now I was living on stress.

My eyes drifted shut, and I blinked to try and rouse myself. Rest was a luxury and a risk, and the lack of it was having predictable repercussions. I couldn't afford to let my guard down, even here on the top of this abandoned warehouse that looked like it hadn't seen human footsteps since the infamous war.

A flashback of the supplier going up in flames brought a familiar surge of hopelessness.

Gone.

No meds for Adam, even assuming I could've gotten them to him.

I had no idea what to do or where to go for more.

I was exhausted with the war and the consequence of humanity's greatest folly. The pendulum was always swinging on progress and regression. Back and forth, back and forth from the day we started to grunt as we scratched pictures into the dirt. *You cannot stop the wheels of progress.* I'd read that in a history book while ensconced within my uncles community and still had time and facility to waste on such pursuits. I couldn't recall the title now, but it covered a thousand years of history through what was called the Dark Ages.

I thought we had set ourselves back a thousand years, maybe more.

Compassion and fundamental human rights were gone, and now every day was colored by survival.

If progress had happened since the collapse, I was too close to the action to see.

And if I didn't get some rest, I was going to make a mistake.

Blaine

"Have we lost many?" Taylor asked, sharp eyes surveying the scene of his making.

"Yeah, some," I replied. "More than I wanted, but you don't assimilate a city without some fallout."

We stood on the rooftop of a recently acquired building, twenty stories of semi-derelict gangland heaven that gave a good vantage of the city. To our north, fires burned uncontrolled, and the light rain offered nothing useful for the cause.

Taylor nodded. The man had not risen to be the leader of two, soon to be three, cities and a dozen towns without an impressive grasp of strategy, and a gut instinct second to none where trouble was concerned.

On the far side of the roof bracing the exit door, two members of his personal security team stood waiting. I was trusted; they were more interested in a potential threat from below.

"You look like shit," Taylor said, side-eyeing me with a grin that was sharp and white against his dark skin. "What's the point in all those enhancements if you still look like shit?"

I shrugged. If I thought about it, I could probably identify the individual layers of bruising that came from the seven days of intense fighting. Things had gotten messy during the operation at a couple of points.

The previous owner of this district wasn't relinquishing possession without a fight.

And a fight was what we'd got.

"Enhancements just mean I can take a lot more shit. Hence I look like, well, whatever." Taylor's comment wasn't one that required a serious response, and to be fair, I was too tired to care.

"We're going to need to take Sanctuary," he said, distracting me from the battered state of my body. The self-proclaimed King's attention had turned south to where the small fortified community stood.

"I figured as much," I replied. Taking a peaceful enclave never sat well. If they wanted to be left alone, it was fine by me. Unfortunately for Sanctuary, they were right in the middle of a pocket of fierce resistance. Peace would be slow to arrive after such a brutal change of ruler. As was inevitable, those previously wielding power here would be kicking up trouble as they sought to wrest control back.

Perhaps Sanctuary had enough supplies to weather out the surrounding storm. Given its defensible structure, there was also a chance that those trouble makers would turn their attention to it as a base. Sanctuary's defense was basic at present, but its layout and composition meant it could be ramped up with relative ease by a motivated party. We didn't need a rebel force holed up in the middle of the city. Better if Sanctuary was in our hands.

Better still if we rendered it to a pile of rubble and removed it from the equation altogether.

Taylor turned to me. "The question is, when?"

That he asked was something. I was more aware than ever after this recent acquisition that the man who called himself a King was not someone who took the time to ask anyone anything.

The troops were going to fucking hate me pressing forward with this tonight, but it needed to be done. After a long, intense week of sporadic sleep and brutal fighting, much of it hand-to-hand, everyone was exhausted. But we were close to the end of the operation, and we all needed some proper rest. "Tonight. It's not going to take a lot to pop the door cannons. The quicker this is over with, the better."

Not that life would be easy after this. There would be pockets of resistance, and constant patrolling of the new territory needed until it stabilized. But once Sanctuary was dealt with, we could withdraw the heavy artillery.

"Keep me informed." Approval given, Taylor turned to leave the rooftop, his silent bodyguards falling into position around him.

The battered metallic roof door rattled shut behind them.

Resigned, I tapped my ear communicator. "All units blue team, we are moving to GF64. Target is a civilian enclave, Sanctuary. Position outside defensive range, and await orders."

The stained concrete walls of Sanctuary looked somber in the night sky. The old data center was mostly windowless, and the only way in or out was the front entrance. Oppressive for its inhabitants, challenging for anyone trying to get in. Nothing moved down there. But as I looked beyond, the heavy artillery came sweeping around the corner at the far end of the street. It felt improbable that these isolated communities survived the surrounding conflict. Certainly, this would not be the first time the city block around it had changed hands. Still, this was the first time that the whole city had come together under a single leader, and while at present that leadership may be tremulous, Taylor's history of conquest suggested it wouldn't stay that way for long.

Chapter Three

Nora

The harsh drone of an alarm sounded throughout the former data center. Jodi and our small combat-trained contingent had returned yesterday after finding a small window in the fighting. Now, she stood beside Mary and me, glaring at the single monitor feed that miraculously continued to function despite the bombardment.

A heavy thud-thud of outbound fire came from the two defense cannons that protected the front entrance. They were taking the kind of explosive hammering that could not be sustained for long, and the whole building rumbled from inbound fire, completing a chaotic symphony of terror.

It was only a matter of time before we were breached.

So far, all our defense had achieved was the destruction of a small armored vehicle, which I was sure was a fuck-up on the part of a tired soldier since it had entered the cannon range. Stupidly, I worried that someone might have gotten hurt, maybe killed. You'd think after seventeen years of this shit, I'd have grown harder. I didn't want them in here. I wanted them far away from me and mine, but I didn't want them dead either.

The smaller guns that focused on the soldiers had been knocked out instantly. In fairness to our protection, it was only intended to deter the lawless outsiders who were uncoordinated at best. A few blasts usually discouraged anyone poking their nose around the entrance. It was clear from the scale of the attack that a big player had decided to end Sanctuary.

"What do they want with us?" Mary demanded.

No one answered.

The scene revealed via the single monitor was the product of nightmares. So many troops it was crazy the way they had converged on little old us. A show of force? They were killing a cockroach with a grenade.

We all had a place in the new world. Couldn't they leave us alone?

Tracer fire and bullets sprayed across the dark sky, the aim centered on the two encased cannons that braced Sanctuary's entrance. Their shields were crumbling critically—they wouldn't last much longer.

"Shut them off," I said flatly, a sense of resignation enveloping me.

"What? Are you fucking crazy?" Jodi demanded. She had been one of Sanctuary's founders and I understood her conflict.

"They're going to fail anyway." I wasn't presenting anything revolutionary here. "It's over, Jodi. We all know it." I held her steady glare. We had to face facts.

It was me who looked away first, my focus shifting to the room beyond the glass partition where Rachel paced with Adam in her arms. The little nine-year-old orphan had an uncanny ability to soothe the crying child. Adam had been screaming when the attack first began. Now, he was miraculously asleep despite the horrendous noise, exhaustion winning out.

"She's right," Mary said. "All we're doing is delaying the inevitable and pissing them off. The cannons won't last. I've not seen anything on this scale for a decade or more. If they wanted in the rough way, we'd be breached already. Look at their weapons." She jabbed a finger at the monitor. "That's professional gear. If it comes to close fighting, then we're all dead. If we offer our surrender, we have a chance."

"A chance?" Jodi spat back bitterly.

"There's nothing more final than dead, Jodi. Anything else is a bonus," Mary said tiredly, words that had become a mantra of sorts. How many times had I heard her say that exact phrase? Too many. "We're all survivors here. Survivors know when to fight and when to lay down and look whipped."

Jodi's sharp gaze settled on the monitor feed. "I can't believe you let Ava leave. What the fuck were you thinking?"

For all I could be blunt, I didn't do anger anymore. I was weak compared to Jodi, and in the new world, strength counted as much as intelligence, perhaps more. Jodi lacked neither but was blinded to reason because Ava was missing. But my son... I could get angry for my son.

Supplies of the medication Adam needed had been sketchy for two months. Although manufacturing had sprung up in some of the larger communities during the intervening years, it didn't always trickle through to the suppliers outside. Jodi and the team had been far from Sanctuary searching for alternative supplies. Then they'd gotten cut off, and the local supplier had sent a message to say they'd received limited numbers. It was first come, first served. The injection lasted a month, but Adam was already overdue. "We needed supplies. We still need supplies. It's been a week since Adam had his last dose. We didn't know where the fuck you all were. Didn't know whether you would be coming back. We had to do something."

My voice broke at the end. I was so fucking helpless and useless, but my baby needed meds. I was crumbling inside and holding myself together by the barest thread. I didn't know what would happen next. If we didn't yield, maybe they would move on. Or perhaps they would storm the place, killing us all. I thought that unlikely given they were targeting only the cannons rather than bombarding the whole building. But selfishly, I thought they might have the medication my son needed. And damn, I'd barter my last breath and freedom to give my baby a chance.

We were all hurting. The lines on Jodi's face reflected all I felt. It was hard to let go and admit defeat. "She'll keep herself safe." I wasn't sure if I was trying to convince myself or Jodi. "We won't help her by getting ourselves killed, and if she's watching, then hopefully she'll follow our lead. We're out of options, Jodi, you know we are." I spoke earnestly and tried to see past my own selfish needs.

Jodi closed her eyes and took a deep breath. "Do it. Shut them off."

Mary hit the button. The sudden absence of the thumping outbound blasts was followed by their response when the inbound bombardment also ceased.

"Turn off the alarm," Jodi growled.

Mary hit the override sending the room into an eerie silence.

No one spoke. I pushed my swivel chair away from the console, my focus shifting to the little girl holding Adam beyond the glass partition. When I turned back, Jodi's face had turned waxy in the emergency lighting.

"Get everyone together in the main room," she said. "Then we'll open the doors."

It was done. Our time in Sanctuary was over, and a new future stretched out to the terrifying unknown.

Ava

The dark, wet streets reflected back foreboding. It hadn't stopped raining, and the constant drizzle soaking into my clothes made them heavy and cold. A fire blazed to my north, the glow lighting the night sky. Smoke drifted sluggishly against the light rain.

I'd been praying for a break in the fighting so I could sneak back into Sanctuary. It hadn't happened, and I could only watch helplessly from the rooftop of a neighboring building as enemy soldiers marched in and out of Sanctuary like ants discovering a new and interesting food source. Whatever the fate of my friends, I could do nothing for them. Our community had been swallowed up by something far larger.

I worried about the thirty individuals who called Sanctuary home—the people I'd come to think of as a family. For a startling, dark moment, I genuinely didn't care about my own fate as I watched this unfold from the vantage of a desolate rooftop.

It had taken years for the nightmares to stop after I fled my former home with Jodi. The last few days had picked me up and thrown me right back into the middle of one. Only this was no nightmare, it was terrifyingly real.

Turning, I sat back against the low wall surrounding the rooftop. Perhaps I would stay here. I was so desperately cold, tired, hungry, and numb that nothing had any purpose or shape anymore.

My eyes must have closed, a light exhausted doze pulling me under. I'd no idea for how long, but when I opened my eyes again, a man was standing before me. He was big, head to toe in black battle fatigues with his face lost in the shadows of a helmet. In that single, heart-stopping glance, I could see he carried enough weapons to start a one-man war.

Time stretched; no thoughts would form.

Then everything slammed back into focus and I fumbled for the Colt. In a lightning-fast move, the weapon was snatched from my grasp as he wrenched me with dizzying speed to my feet.

"What the fuck is this?" he demanded, voice a low growl as he fisted my right arm in an iron grip. I dangled, my toes scraping over the rough stone floor as I fought to regain my footing. He examined the gun with a shake of his head. "Rust. Like real fucking rust."

I'd spent an unhealthy amount of time since I left Sanctuary, regaling my tired mind with horror-filled scenarios pertaining to my capture. Reality matched most of them. In most, I'd attempted to fire it or managed a few moves before defeat.

He tossed my former weapon to the floor as though utterly disgusted by its presence. Finally, some shred of training clicked, and my fist slammed into his throat.

A sharp pain shot the length of my arm. My stomach turned over at the choked gurgling noise he made. Releasing me, he doubled over, coughing.

I was off, sprinting toward the fire exit door without a backward glance. The thud of my footsteps reverberated through my body while my racing heart pounded in my ears. My vision tunneled on that door. I became mindless to everything but the need to flee, my throat so dry that my breath shuttled in and out with a hoarse rasp.

He was giving chase—his heavier footsteps gaining on me, driving my animal instinct to scramble for options.

There were none. I was closing in on the door, but he was gaining on me.

The world turned grey. Within reach of my grasping fingers, the door became an irrational hope given there were many floors to descend. Yet still, I gripped the handle and yanked.

It opened an inch, then crashed shut as the impact of my body smacked into the flat, hard surface due to a body plowing into me from behind. A short, sharp, terrorized scream escaped my lips, after which I could neither breathe nor move. My head rattled from the blow of my forehead connecting with unyielding metal before I was spun around and slammed back against the door.

I slid a little, legs planted wide, my whole body shaking and limp as the adrenaline abandoned me in the wake of shock and pain.

Stepping back, he coughed hard, snatching at the fastener on his helmet before ripping it off.

Dropping it carelessly to the floor, he massaged his throat. The rain had stopped, and the wind whipped up, sending his dark hair swirling around his face. His features were in the shadows, giving an impression of rugged lines that solidified as he turned to face me.

Eyes as dark as the night sky, handsome, forbidding, and utterly furious.

"How long have you been running?" His voice was gruff, from the blow most likely, and the question surprised me given his eyes spat death threats.

The truth or a lie? "A few days," I said, unable to formulate anything more useful than the truth. A headache was radiating from my forehead and everything was spinning.

"And hiding up here?" he demanded.

I should be searching for an opening to attack, but my head

felt like it was no longer connected to me, and he was watching me closely enough that another lucky punch was unlikely.

"A few days."

He huffed out a breath as he took a step closer, cautiously as though expecting me to pull a move—it took all my focus to remain upright.

He wasn't going to hurt me. Instinct told me monsters did not ask about your situation... especially after you'd just punched them. I squirmed a little as he caught my chin between strong fingers, turning my face to expose it to the limited light.

The barest tightening of his fingers told me he'd noticed my skin held no mark.

"You're going to need an owner," he said.

My stomach turned over slowly, my world contracted and then expanded, heart rate surging within my chest.

I nodded.

"You know how this works?" He released my chin, running his fingers down my throat until they rested at the base, collaring me. The light pressure held a warning. Thoughts escaped my grasp as I became hyper-aware of our size difference, of his strength, of my helplessness. His fingers were warm against my cold skin—I'd gotten chilled to the bone in my wet clothing.

Ownership.

That word was like ice water, bringing a sluggish surge of fresh fear. He shifted his stance, thumb grazing the flesh before dipping into my pulse point.

"Yes, I think so."

His lips narrowed to a line. "Then consider it done."

My vision turned to sparkling dots. It would hurt when I hit the floor, but thankfully by the time it happened I was already unconscious.

Chapter Four

Blaine

I caught her before she hit the ground. Shock, exhaustion, or the blow to her head?

Three days hiding with no evidence of a backpack was a long time to go without supplies, definitely exhaustion. The way her pulse had leaped at the mention of ownership, definitely shock.

A bruise was forming on her forehead, but she sounded lucid—until she fainted dead away.

Yeah, what the fuck did I know? Hoisting her limp body over one shoulder, I opened the fire exit and headed down the stairs.

What had possessed me to offer ownership? I could do without the added responsibility. Yet, she reminded me of something that I hadn't witnessed in a long while, something I couldn't even quantify.

Reservations aside, I headed for ground level, stepping over rubble and navigating collapsed ceilings. The building was a derelict shell, and a death trap, and of no interest to anyone; hence why we'd given it no more than a cursory check.

Perhaps I could find someone half-decent who wanted a bed-warmer? She was a mess now, but might be reasonable enough once the grime and fatigue were gone.

She weighed next to nothing. How did something so fragile even survive? I swore under my breath as I trudged down the stairs, knowing I wasn't going to pass her off. Not until I'd spoken to her properly. It was obvious that she was inadequately equipped to survive the real world. So why the burning curiosity?

Maybe it was because I could still remember the world before the war. Or perhaps she reminded me that there was more to a woman than the hardness most were driven to. There were still a few baubles, the pretty ones that needed powerful men to keep them safe, but they soon gained a different type of hardness.

The woman swinging over my shoulder was so far out of her fucking depth, it was borderline obscene. When was the last time I'd witnessed that?

My lips twitched. Yeah, and the little wildcat had still disabled me like a pro. I must be more tired than I thought.

As I hit ground level, I stalked straight for the medical van where Carter would be found. No one paid me any heed, and if they did, they knew better than to interfere.

"Got an emergency," I stated. A soldier sat on the stretcher in the back of the van. Carter looked up while continuing to dispense the contents of a syringe into the man's arm. Blood splattered the soldier's fatigues, and an ugly pink, just-sealed scar ran the length of his forearm.

The soldier glanced up, then nearly gave himself whiplash as he sought something riveting in the rows of neat, white storage that lined the ambulance wall.

Carter's gaze shifted to the body over my shoulder. He raised a brow before dismissing the soldier. "You're good to go."

The grunt exited like he had a burning need to be elsewhere.

I dumped the limp woman on the vacant stretcher. In the bright lights of the med-van, her face was pale and grubby. She appeared even smaller on that stretcher sized to take a soldier. Her tight woolen hat was sodden, and her clothing was equally wet.

Carter pressed his fingers over her pulse point as he held a scanner to her forehead. "What happened?"

"Exhaustion, I think. She was talking when I found her. Said she had been in the warehouse for a few days." I thumbed over my shoulder. "No supplies with her that I saw. I'm presuming she's from Sanctuary or knew them. I noticed someone on the rooftop watching. I was expecting a sniper or a ganger snooping. Not a lone woman fit to collapse. Banged her head against a door."

That part was down to me. In my defense, she had just throat-punched me with a surprisingly fierce, bony little fist.

Carter nodded, snagging a syringe and a vial from a drawer. "Pulse is fine, and no signs of anything like an infection, no temperature, breathing steady. Lack of consciousness is a worry." Taking scissors, he cut her sleeve away before filling a syringe.

"I need ownership on this one," I said.

Carter's head snapped around, whatever he'd intended to do momentarily forgotten.

"You killed her owner?" He turned her face to the side. He froze. The sodden hat was ripped from her head like the mark might be hiding underneath. In the stark lighting, the lack of branding was evident. "She doesn't have an owner," he stated, pinning me with a steady gaze loaded with unspoken questions.

"I'm well aware of that. Put my mark on her." I ran my fingers through my damp hair. I'd left my helmet on the rooftop. Now I'd have Inventory all over my ass, making me write a report. I wasn't going back to get it. I'd already spent far too many hours and days running up and down the stairs of derelict buildings.

"Blaine, you don't need me to explain the rules of ownership to you. But just to be crystal clear, you cannot put your mark on a free woman. If she already had a mark, that's a different story, but she doesn't, and there are procedures. There would need to be a hearing—others may have a prior claim."

"Do I look like I give a fuck?" My tone was sharp. "This isn't a discussion. Put the mark on her and let me deal with any consequence."

He cursed and shook his head as though fighting with internal demons. "You're asking a lot," he stated, pushing the needle into her upper arm. "Are you asking this as my brother? Or my dickhead brother who's going to get us both killed?"

I tried not to smile, but it slipped out. "Probably the latter." I thought it unlikely anyone would push the issue of her ownership. Taylor wouldn't be interested in pissing me off since I was useful to his domination plans. A few of his influential minions might take an interest in stirring shit up, but I'd deal with them if the need arose.

The only people who dared to give me grief were the muppets in Inventory. What was one woman? We'd picked up dozens of people over the last seven days. They'd be assimilated into Taylor's world. Those who'd lost their owner would be allocated a new one... if it hadn't already happened. "You telling me no one has asked you to set ownership since this little foray began? Anything worth keeping gets snapped up. They put their mark on it damn quick."

"They already had owners," Carter gritted out. "You know

the kind of woman who doesn't have a mark? The kind that's going to be trouble. The kind that removed it or never had it. She either is or was connected to someone powerful—is that clear enough for you?"

"Put my mark on her."

He growled, the little asshole, I ought to smack him up the side of the head.

"Did she agree to this? Have you even asked her or told her?" he persisted, tossing the used needle into a red plastic container.

I shrugged. "Kind of, then she passed out. Something tells me she's not the outdoor type."

"So we can safely assume she was either responding under duress or was delirious and will have no recollection of what the hell she said. Why are you taking this on?"

"Carter, you know what's going to happen if we leave her to the vultures? You wanna see her with Harris? Or one of Taylor's other 'yes' men? No one fucking deserves that. Why am I taking responsibility? I've no idea, to be honest. I couldn't leave her half-dead on the rooftop, and I'm not ready to walk away."

He nodded once. Lips forming a grim line, he withdrew the chain from his neck. The brander hung from the end. He configured it to match the brand on my right temple before pressing it to her left temple. The tattoo was permanent. It could only be replaced using another brander, and access to those was strictly controlled.

A strange, undefinable emotion rolled through me seeing my mark on her flesh.

"It's done," he said, stirring me from my rumination. "You want to leave me to deal with her medical problems now?" It wasn't a question, and I didn't want to push my luck.

"Sure, message me when she comes to." I hopped down

from the med-van. Then stopped and turned back. "Better fit her with a tracker."

He growled.

Asshole. I smirked.

"Fine, I'll fit her with a tracker. Already bit the bullet. What's one more transgression?"

He continued to mutter to himself as he began dragging equipment out of drawers. Chances were she'd wake up soon. I fully expected Carter to let me know when he was ready and not a moment before.

Chapter Five

Carter

After Blaine left, I directed the driver to head back to Guilder City. The main assault was over, and I was no longer needed on the ground.

On the way to the medical center, I ran some basic tests—nothing of immediate concern. She was sleepy, a little disorientated, fatigued, and dehydrated, but doing well, all things considered.

Once we arrived at the medical center, further tests revealed several interesting enhancements to her glands, along with cell renewal and rejuvenation. She also bore the kind of lean musculature that suggested an optimized metabolism—all expensive stuff. There was little doubt that she was once someone important, possibly still was given her lack of branding.

I wasn't one for questioning Blaine, not in a serious way. He was my older brother. I'd still been a kid when the collapse happened. The preceding years weren't pretty either. Violence bubbled up everywhere, curfews were part of everyday life, but we had clung to the pretense of normality.

Blaine was an experienced veteran of several of the bloodiest pre-collapse wars. I'd been on the streets living rough when he found me. I still don't know how.

My chances of survival without him had been small.

But today, and for the first time, I was questioning his decision regarding the grubby waif who lay unconscious on the medical cot.

The nurse had just called me over after informing me that Blaine's property was showing marked signs of improvement.

Ownership. That word left an aftertaste in my mouth. Blaine had never indicated that he might consider it before, and now he was leaping headfirst with an ownerless woman who was going to get him killed.

I braced myself for a scream as she opened her eyes—she'd been a little out of it when we'd last spoke. Women ended up in medical for all kinds of reasons. Most were traumatic. Screaming, ranting, and attempted flight were all usual reactions. And she was strapped to the bed—a necessary precaution in light of those reactions, but one that could lead to a response all of its own.

No scream came. The slightest frown accompanied her trying to move and finding her wrists bound.

"How are you feeling?" I asked, a well-practiced distraction from her restrained pose while I assessed her mental state. A couple of guards hovered close at hand should I need help. Not that I needed any help with one tiny woman who was weakened from an ordeal.

She blinked a few times before her steady gaze found mine.

"Do you remember what happened?" I asked. The eyes staring back at me were a luminous winter blue that put her genetic level work into a whole other category and instantly piqued my scientific interest. Such modifications had been cutting edge pre-war, and post-war the focus had been military based for good reasons.

"Yes, I do." Her brows drew together again as she subtly tested the restraints. Despite a couple of applications with the medical scanner, a shiny, raised bruise marred the center of her forehead. "I think." She froze as she noticed the two hulking guards.

I waved them away, and despite feeling I hadn't had enough time to fully assess her, ripped the velcro fasteners open. "Not everyone wakes up as composed as you," I said.

She shuffled to a sitting position. Her fingers searched the small egg on her forehead—she winced. "Where am I?"

"Guilder medical center," I said, noting how she stilled. "Can you tell me your name and the last thing you remember?"

Her expressive eyes shifted from me to the drip attached to her arm before settling on her dirt streaked fingers. She toyed with the soft white blanket a nurse had placed over her.

"Ava. I was on the roof of the old Coaster warehouse talking to a man. I fainted."

I didn't press her for a surname, tapping the information into the datapad. Most new citizens gave a false name or nothing at all. Besides, I was a doctor. My job was to note the basics if they offered them and let others further down the processing line worry about the rest. "That man asked me to give you his mark."

Her fingers stilled. "Did you?" Impossibly colored eyes searched mine.

I nodded. "Yes, I did." She didn't blink for the longest time, and her fingers turned white around the blanket.

"I understand," she said.

"Is there someone else you would prefer as a guardian?" It felt a lot like betrayal asking that question, but I had to know how deep this was about to go. No one in Taylor's patch had guardianship rights. But he had agreements of sorts with other warlords. I guess anything was possible given the absence of a mark.

The tiny shake of her head didn't relieve me as much as I'd hoped. "No, there is no one," she said quietly.

Blaine was big enough and bad enough to manage his own bullshit. His claim was already on her. Several people had seen it and commented. I needed to stop asking probing questions when I wouldn't know what to do with the answers. "Let me remove the drip, and you can have some liquid food." I removed the cannula before pressing a clean cotton ball over the tiny hole.

"Sanctuary? Do you know?"

That answered where she was from. It also made me curious as to how an unmarked woman had stumbled into our midst.

"It's gone," I said. No point in allowing her to harbor any hopes of returning there. "The community will be treated fairly." A lot depended on the people themselves and their acceptance of their new situation. I wanted to offer more; there was a compelling innocence to her demeanor that sparked an urge to provide false comforts. There'd been plenty of women who'd come and gone from Blaine's life, but I could see why this one had stirred his protective cavemen side.

Okay, so they were women owned by someone else—men liked to offer them up as favors to Blaine. It was fair to say the women didn't mind, either.

"Can I see them?"

"Ah, no. Any prior ownership would be respected, and family relationships considered. Do you meet those criteria?"

Her lashes lowered again, shoulders sloped. "It's a small

community. They were like a family to me. But no, none meet that criteria."

"Then I must let Blaine know you're ready to be collected. There's time for you to take a shower first if you feel up to it."

"Definitely, yes, please." Her enthusiasm for the shower was understandable given the dirt caking the exposed parts of her body. I just hoped the meltdown I was anticipating could be staved off until Blaine arrived.

Ava

They gave me a disgusting drink that left my stomach strangely full and yet empty. When I didn't throw up—I think they were concerned that I might—they took me to a shower room and left me to the task.

I'd heard of Guilder City. It wasn't so far from my former home, and I recalled my uncle mentioning it a time or two. I wish I'd paid more attention now. Still, that was several years ago, and a lot could happen in that time.

The doctor who tended me possessed the kind of boyish good looks that bordered on beauty. He was politely kind in his treatment of me, perhaps in deference to my new owner. The nurse had called him Doctor Carter. It could have been his first name or surname. Who knew the usual way to address a doctor in this post-war world.

Was he even a doctor? It wasn't as if there were medical schools anymore. He looked to be in his twenties, and would have been a child when the collapse occurred.

Not that any of this mattered. He'd seemed competent enough, and that was the length and breadth of my interest.

As I'd stood on that desolate rooftop, I'd known I was out of options. Finding the new community wasn't complete chaos was a bonus.

Stripping from my filthy clothes, I got under the spray. The water was hot, and I felt human again as I watched the grime disappear down the drain hole. I scrubbed myself in the apple scented gel, got a good dollop in my hair, and scrubbed at that as well. While I washed, I didn't need to think about what would happen next.

Three days... how had I survived three days?

How would I survive what came next? I wanted to shut down the fears, but my thoughts would not be contained. They were restless, instantly shifting to worry about Nora and Adam. Were they here? They must be. Carter had said my former community would be treated fairly. This medical facility was far beyond anything I'd seen since the war. They would have the medication Adam needed, I was sure.

I tried valiantly to force blank into my mind between these pockets of worry, and to not let myself drift into a dangerous, painful zone, but it was a fruitless endeavor.

Jodi.

A physical pain settled in my gut, the wound, too raw to touch, and yet my mind honed in on it regardless. I stood motionless beneath the spray, dazed by the enormity of my situation. It didn't seem real that this was happening and that Jodi was gone from my life. This new path that opened up before me was unexpected and frightening. It wasn't what I wanted—it wasn't fair. Nothing ever was.

I wouldn't allow fear to consume me. Now was not the time to wallow in self-pity. I had to focus on surviving and be strong.

Jodi would be fine; she was so fucking tough. She wouldn't do anything foolish. We could bide our time until we got an understanding of this community and how it all worked. We were survivors, and we did what we had to do today so that we were still here tomorrow.

I could still remember vividly the day my uncle introduced her to me as my personal bodyguard after the previous one tried to rape me. My uncle thought Jodi the safer option because she was a woman. In some ways, she was—no one touched me again. But he also underestimated the way that we would bond.

That was his first mistake. Jodi had kept me safe, and I'd hero-worshiped her long before we'd fled. And after... she had demonstrated herself worthy of my respect and adoration a thousand times over.

She won't do anything stupid. Nothing was more final than death, we could bide our time, and both flee once again.

The water pelted me as I shied away from the burgeoning conclusion.

Yeah, Jodi was going to do something very stupid.

I took a deep breath as my tears mingled with the water rushing over my body. Another deep breath and I willed myself to let it go. I finished the shower under automation until my skin turned pink and a little wrinkly. Flipping the shower off, I rubbed myself dry.

They had given me some clean clothes: ugly grey fatigue pants, a black T-shirt, and my old black boots. The pants and the top were too large, not that I cared. The thin plastic comb was a kind gesture, and I ran it through my hair before placing it back on the chair.

After, I simply waited, stalling, yet not ready to open the door. What had I done? What was I going to do?

Not thinking about it was the only answer I had. This was out of my hands now and beyond my limited control. The community of Sanctuary had been an escape that had lasted longer than any of us could have hoped, and I was grateful for that time.

Bracing myself, I opened the door, surprised that no one was standing waiting on the other side.

A nurse approached, smiling as she noticed me. A mark of ownership was visible at her temple, yet she appeared happy, even relaxed. Could this place be so terrible when an owned woman was comfortable enough to smile? "Oh my goodness! You look so different without all that dirt."

I winced and wished the dirt back as she ushered me toward the foyer, where she said, "Doctor Carter is waiting."

Doctor Carter was indeed waiting. Only he wasn't alone.

I came to an abrupt stop since my new owner was standing no more than three paces away. *Blaine.* I presumed that was his name after Carter mentioned it. He had his back to me as he stood talking to Carter... Carter, who did a double-take on noticing me.

Whatever they had been conversing about—I suspected it might have been me—was forgotten in the wake of Carter's riveted interest. As was inevitable, the man who now owned me turned around.

His gaze was steady. Nothing flickered, no surprise, or anything else for that matter, just a dark, endless look that rooted me to the spot and stopped and started my heart like someone had cranked up electrodes. He looked like some futuristic god of war. Even as poetically dramatic as that sounded, I couldn't retract the notion. His face held a carnal beauty surrounded by dark, disheveled hair that fell to his collar. There was bruising along his jawline, his right cheekbone, and his left eye was turning black—the evidence of his lifestyle. If his face looked this bad, I wondered about the rest.

The fatigues were gone, but he was still dressed all in black with a long, full-length duster and a personal arsenal in evidence. He radiated vitality, both from his size and some inner presence that stated he was someone to be reckoned with. It hardly seemed possible that this was the same man I'd met on the rooftop and had winded with a blow.

His lips twitched; I wondered if he was replaying that same event. His smile faded as quickly as it arrived, his expression turned to stone, and his lips formed a line.

"Not quite what I was expecting," he said in a deep, rough voice—maybe it wasn't the blow after all.

Chapter Six

Blaine

I'd known she was going to be trouble. But as I studied the scrubbed-up version of my acquisition, I realized it was a different kind of trouble to the one I'd first anticipated. Take me back to the rooftop, and this time I'd leave her there.

"Well, if anyone can—" Carter left the sentence hanging. *Dickhead*.

He was still staring at Ava—if that really was her name—and all he was missing was the slack jaw. I drew a measured breath and willed myself not to react, which was hard considering she must have always gotten some kind of reaction. Even the drab, oversized clothing only seemed to emphasize her slender frame and beauty. Carter muttered something about needing to take samples for his genetics research. The words barely registered. My lips tugged up as I recalled her planting her tiny fist in my windpipe. She looked like she couldn't survive a strong wind, let alone three days outside.

"Not quite what I was expecting," I said. Not even close.

It was too late. My mark was at her temple. Her damp hair obscured it a little, but it still brought a tightening to my gut. "Time to go," I said. My voice was sharper than I intended—I was trying to work out a scenario where I didn't spend my days bloody defending what was mine. Keeping her locked in my apartment twenty-four-seven became an enticing option.

Her breath hitched. I'd come straight from a debrief with Taylor and was loaded to the hilt with weapons. She looked like an angel—I was closer to nightmare material. My face was a mess, my body no better, although at least the evidence of the abuse was hidden behind layers of clothing.

There was a mental delay before she figured that was her cue to join me. When she finally got her ass moving, it was with such obvious reluctance that my irritation surged. The quicker she got used to her situation, the better. Her time in Sanctuary had been an unsustainable trip into a fantasy world. Reality, even in the semi-civilized Guilder City, was dark and brutal. That I was better than most of the men she might have ended up with would be of little comfort—not that she knew that.

Still, I hadn't asked for this, hadn't expected to find a woman standing on that rooftop, or to suffer this sense of responsibility. I could have walked away. I still wondered why I hadn't.

The role of ownership was new to me. There had been neither reason nor desire to consider it before, and besides, it had always seemed wrong. Now that I found myself participating, there an element of self-loathing that could not entirely mask my curiosity. By law, she belonged to me, was mine to do with as I pleased, within reason, yet I was forced to admit the concept wasn't as uncomfortable as I expected.

It felt right. Like it was the natural order of things. Yeah, that was pretty fucked up.

Her eyes were everywhere but on me; she thanked Carter

and shook his hand while bestowing on him a kind smile. He reciprocated with a practiced charm that usually left any woman in the vicinity swooning. I was going to kick the little prick's ass when we were next alone.

"You can let go now, Carter," I said, settling a proprietary hand on the back of her neck. Her dark hair was almost dry and felt silky soft under my rough fingers. Carter retained possession of her hand longer than was polite, obviously intending to provoke me further.

She didn't pull away from me, but her stiffness made it clear she wasn't enjoying the touch, which pissed me off.

Carter watched on, smirking as we exited the building. Turning back, I mouthed, *asshole,* as I steered her through the door.

I'd parked my Humvee directly outside the building; the guards on watch at the hospital dipped their heads as I passed. Opening the passenger door, I put her inside, slammed the door, and rounded the vehicle to the driver's side.

"There was no need to be unkind to him."

My door had barely clunked shut, and I paused the key not yet in the ignition and struggling to assimilate what I'd heard.

I glanced across to find her staring at me. A tiny little frown marred her perfect little forehead above a perfect little nose, and two impossibly luminous eyes regarded me with contempt.

"Ava, I'm more than happy to hand you over to the nice doctor, if that's what you want." The frown disappeared, and her eyes widened. "Not sure how long he'll survive with the kind of trouble a woman like you will bring, though." Her eyes narrowed, and I congratulated myself on my amazing lack of tact.

"A woman like me?"

Her voice had a measured softness that immediately took my mind to the gutter. I eased position in the seat and tried to ignore how her lips appeared to be both the perfect fullness and the perfect shade of pink. "Let's face it, you're going to attract attention, and out here, in the real world, guys like Carter are going to end up looking like roadkill when someone decides to pursue ownership the uncivilized way."

She blinked a few times. "You mean like you did?"

My wildcat had a mouth. Where the fuck had this other persona been hiding? Someone should have put a warning label on her sassy ass.

"The nice Doctor looked more than capable of handling himself," she added.

That pissed me off on so many levels I couldn't decide which one took precedence. "I made the offer, and you accepted, as I seem to recall." I scrubbed a hand through my hair and wondered where the fuck this conversation was going.

"I was half-starved and desperate. What else was I going to do?" Her tone had risen ever so slightly, and I became aware that we were still sitting outside the hospital and were doubtless drawing attention. "You must be a veritable saint. Forgive me for not noticing."

Damn, the woman had a tongue that could cut through reinforced steel. If I'd been somewhere more private, I'd be putting her over my knee and swatting that no doubt perfect little ass. I was still considering it... "You want to look for a better offer?" I turned in the seat to face her, confused about why I asked this question and wondering what the fuck I'd do if she called my bluff.

She looked away, facing straight ahead in a way that said the conversation was over.

My anger drained. I felt fucking guilty and then angry for feeling guilty when I had no reason to be.

"I may understand the world we live in," she said softly. "But I don't have to like it."

I mentally tacked the word *asshole* on the end because it was clearly what she was thinking. Ramming the key in the ignition, I fired up the engine.

Ava

The journey passed in silence. What was wrong with me? Why had I provoked him? I knew absolutely nothing about the man, and here I was, trapped in a car with him, headed for a destination and fate unknown.

I needed my head examined. Maybe I'd hit the door harder than I thought?

And my fate wasn't entirely unknown. Certain things were a given, expected even. My wild rant was probably my fear manifesting in an obscure, and with hindsight, dangerous way. Whatever my personal feelings toward the man brooding silently beside me, I knew better than to act out.

Sanctuary was part of my history. I was no longer in the safety and isolation the community had offered. I had to be alert to my owner as a threat.

That he hadn't yet resorted to violence was some comfort; that he was probably considering handing me over to someone who would, was not.

The silence stretched, and the dark, damp streets flashing by through the windows spoke of looming trouble. I should apologize. A delayed sense of self-preservation dictated I salvage what I could. That such a declaration did not sit well, that I still possessed stubborn pride could only be to my detriment. My fingers fidgeted with the oversized T-shirt, screwing it up until I'd twisted it into a knot.

"I'm sorry," I said. "I shouldn't have spoken that way. It won't happen again."

He made no response, appearing focused on the road. Had he heard me?

His glance swept over me before returning to the road. "You probably shouldn't make any wild declarations that you're not going to be able to keep," he said, lips tugging up in a smirk.

Inside, a tiny bud of hope unfurled, a reassertion of my instincts back on that desolate rooftop that said he was someone I could trust. "I'm not very good at this," I said, wondering at my own cryptic words whether I was referring to being around men, being humble, or both.

His laugh had a pleasant timbre, which only added further insult to him laughing at my expense.

He turned off the main road, making a sharp right before pulling to a stop beside a guard post. Here he dipped the blacked-out driver window to show the guard his face.

"Evening, sir," the soldier said. The steel gates immediately clattered open to grant access. Beyond the gates stood a high rise building, all cold grey stone and glass. The grounds surrounding it were heavily patrolled by soldiers with dogs, while enough artillery perched on the surrounding walls to deter anything less than an army.

We passed through another mesh gate into the building's basement where he turned into a parking space. The garage was mostly empty other than a couple of cars and a small truck. Only half the lights worked, casting weak illumination that barely combated the shadows.

He exited the car.

I took a deep breath, heart hammering as a sense of detachment enveloped me. I jumped when my door was flung open, and I stared up at the man who now owned me.

Somehow I got out, and put one foot in front of the other as we headed toward an elevator centering the back wall.

It arrived with a cheery bong that insulted my fraught state. The magnitude of my situation became a debilitating pressure.

What am I doing?

When I remained rooted, he took my arm and drew me inside with him. Pressing his thumb to a print recognition plate, he selected a floor. The elevator creaked as we rose. I hadn't been in one for years and the experience of being enclosed in a metal box combined with his looming presence beside me threatened to induce a panic attack.

The elevator stopped before my hysteria could peak, two floors from the top. Sensor lights flickered on, revealing a corridor with plush, carpeted flooring, and polished wooden doors that stretched both directions. We went right, stopping at an indistinctive door where he used his thumbprint again to give access to an apartment.

Diffused lighting cast over a spacious open plan living area, making a reflection in the soaring window-walls. The layout reminded me of my parents' penthouse in Manhattan, but the similarity ended there. My mother's preference for soft neutral tones was overwritten by strong dark tones and opulence that felt obscene when the state of the world at large was considered.

Abandoning me at the entry, Blaine stalked deeper inside.

Who was this man?

Discarding his duster over a low couch, another thumbprint plate revealed a drawer in the paneled wall. Here he systematically off-loaded and stored his weapons. Far more than I had previously noticed, slid, slipped, and slotted from his person into the hidden space. Task complete, the panel silently closed.

"You want something to eat?" As he turned to face me

again, my stomach flipped over. "The answer you're looking for is—yes, Blaine, I do."

I didn't feel hungry. Shock had me in a stranglehold of confusion, hanging somewhere between full-blown panic and exhaustion.

"Yes, Blaine, I do." His name felt odd on my tongue, but he no longer felt like a stranger, as though speaking that single word could shift us between one state and the next.

"And your name would be?" He started walking back to me, slow, unhurried steps until he was once more directly before me.

"Ava."

He nudged his head to me. "That your real name?"

"It's the name I assumed—after I left a bad situation. It's who I am now."

He nodded. "Blaine is the name my parents gave me, but I guess we don't all take the same path through the apocalypse."

His strength meant his journey through the war should have been easier, but as I looked at his face and the evidence of violence written in cuts and bruises, I thought none of us had had an easy path.

He held out a hand, and I placed mine in his, watching as it was swallowed by his larger one and steeling myself against the strange lightness that invaded me. "Pleased to meet you, Ava. Come in and take a seat."

Chapter Seven

Nora

I'd never seen a medical facility like the one at Guilder City. Even those fleeting childhood memories offered no point of reference. It seemed incredible that such a thing could exist when you considered how much destruction had taken place.

Adam and I had been placed in a large open ward. They'd pulled the screen across so I couldn't see much of the other beds, but I could hear the occasional moan, and ten minutes ago the old lady in the next bed had been noisily puking her guts out.

Adam was lying in a clear plastic cot to the right of my chair with so many cables and monitors attached that my poor boy better resembled a machine than a baby. They'd resolved his medical condition, a simple procedure, I was told. It was a lot to take in, and nothing short of miraculous that his dependency on medication had been erased. That they would help us without demanding something made no sense to my abused perspective of the world.

I was bracing for the demands and fully expected I was about to face a life of servitude.

When I glanced up from my silent study of my baby boy, it was to see the doctor striding toward the nurses' station. His name was Carter. Surname or first name, I didn't know. He looked too young to be a doctor. I seemed to recall doctors being older with steel grey hair and glasses. Still, the man did seem competent, and he had cured my son.

Allegedly.

My focus returned to Adam. No, he was cured; I could sense it. When he needed an injection, his skin took on a sickly tinge, and he cried all the time.

Remembering what had happened made my heart flip a distressed beat. If the attack hadn't happened, and if Sanctuary hadn't fallen, then my son would still be gravely ill. I'd been hysterical with my demands by the time they'd ordered us to exit the building. Jodi tried her best to keep me civil, fearing I was about to get a bullet in my head. But I'd marched up to the nearest soldier, poked him in the chest, and ordered him to get the person in charge because my baby was ill.

I'd been brought to the medical center in a small military SUV. Hardly caring that I was being separated from everyone I'd known for the last year.

I didn't believe in fate; I didn't believe in God either, but forces more powerful than my human comprehension were behind this.

When I turned back, I realized the doctor was heading directly toward me. There was no threat to be found in the floppy-haired doctor with his startling green eyes. But he was a man, and saving my son would buy him no charity.

"He's doing exceptionally well," the doctor stated as he

checked the machine my son's cables were attached to. Carter had a mild, even tone that instilled calm until I remembered—how could I even forget—that he was a man.

A man with ridiculously floppy brown hair that made him appear younger than any credible doctor ought to be.

My relief in hearing this confirmation of Adam's recovery combated against a determination that Doctor Carter couldn't possibly know what he was talking about.

"How old are you?" I demanded. I was renowned for my blunt-talking, as Jodi would attest. But this was rude, even for me.

The doctor's eyes widened before a low, warm, and entirely masculine chuckle escaped him. He was so self-assured and relaxed.

"I'm twenty-six," he stated evenly, lips tugging up in a smile. "Don't worry. I assure you my qualifications are in order."

I looked away from his perceptive green eyes. "Do you even remember the world before the war?" My tone was still combative. I'd been a teenager when my world was ripped into pieces. This relaxed specimen of disturbingly pretty manhood had been a boy. He probably couldn't even remember how dark those years immediately following the war had been. I remembered, and I hated that he didn't.

"And how old are you?" He glanced at his datapad for the information. "Nora?" He smiled before returning his attention to the compact screen. "Ah, the grand age of thirty-two. Those six years must have made you incredibly wise."

Was he making fun of me? I didn't like jokes, and I enjoyed being the object of other people's amusement even less. How dare he make light of this.

He was a man, I reminded myself, and the world was a different place for men.

"There have been no complications with the procedure, and I expect your son to make a full recovery. Another twenty-four hours, and you'll be good to go." His tone remained light and professional.

Yesterday, I'd been sick with worry. Jodi had returned without the medication for Adam. Ava was missing—Ava was still missing, but I needed to deal with one problem at a time.

Today, Adam was no longer a worry—Adam was well. I would never again need to fear for where or how I would acquire his next dose of medication. A slightly less fraught future stretched ahead of me. If only we could go back to our lives.

That wasn't going to happen because there was no longer a home—no longer a Sanctuary.

I'd heard the explosion as we'd raced away in the SUV. When I'd glanced back, the entire front entrance and ten stories above were collapsing into dust and rubble.

The damage was irreparable.

Eyes filled with hatred fixed upon the doctor. "Go where?" I snapped. "You destroyed my home, remember." I had no idea where my words kept coming from. But something about Doctor Carter brought out the Irish temper in me.

His countenance shuttered. "Do I look like a soldier?"

Maybe Doctor Carter hadn't personally destroyed my home, but his people had. He may not be a soldier, but he was a long way from the weakling category, filling out the neatly pressed white shirt in a way that spoke of lean muscle bulk. And who even owned a white shirt anymore? His choice of clothing was as ridiculous as his floppy brown hair.

"You will be given accommodation and your citizenship reviewed," he said coolly. "I cannot say what will happen after."

He began tapping notes on his datapad, expression closed

like another person had invaded his body. The carefree doctor was gone—the transition made me feel strangely sad.

I couldn't do this, couldn't be around men, especially handsome, carefree ones.

"I'll let the allocations team know that you're ready to be interviewed," he stated before turning away.

I watched him stride purposely down the corridor. A nurse stopped him, and he greeted her interruption with a smile before nodding at whatever she was telling him so earnestly. They both left together, disappearing behind another screen.

For the first time in many months, I no longer felt the urge to cry. A weight had been lifted, and in its place was a bereft kind of numb.

Carter

"Doctor Carter, could you have a look at 21C please," the young nurse asked. "She's complaining about stomach pains."

I nodded. "Let's have a look."

I went through the process of checking the patient. Once done, and she had been given some additional pain relief, my thoughts returned to the feisty redhead who'd given me a dressing down. She wasn't the first person to express some incredulity at me being a doctor. Most new arrivals to Taylor's home city were surprised by both the facility and the staff competence.

Life had been rough before we'd been assimilated into the self-proclaimed King's world. Taylor had an IQ off the charts and was certainly no pushover physically. He'd only claimed Guilder City when we arrived. But he already had expansion plans and was investing in roles beyond a person's ability to fight. Blaine and I had both been tested and assessed to see where we might add value.

Blaine was an obvious fit for the forces with his military background, although there was a lengthy probation period where he was watched. Meanwhile, I was shunted into the medical training program. It wasn't what I wanted to do. I'd grown tough over the years we'd been on our own, and I wanted to follow Blaine.

Taylor didn't tolerate any insubordination. You got on board with his decisions, or you were kicked out. Blaine had taken me aside and threatened to kick my ass if I didn't get in line. He might be my brother, and might be prepared to lay his life down to protect me, but he had zero tolerance for my bullshit. I was eleven at the time, full of belligerence and attitude as I moved toward adulthood. With hindsight, I'd needed a firm hand. The soldiering life wasn't easy. The lower ranks were expendable. You proved yourself, or you died trying. Blaine was lucky that he'd been trained, but it was rough in those first years.

I'd had to watch Blaine return from operations battered and bruised only to get up and do the same the next day. He told me to knuckle down with my studies so I didn't have to do the same.

And I had.

But Blaine was intelligent, and he hadn't stayed a grunt for long. Over the years, they had given him genetic enhancements, investing in the best to make them better. He was a tough soldier with a keen sense of operational strategy. By the time Taylor was done, Blaine had had every upgrade a body could handle and took point on leading all the major operations.

The thing about Taylor was that he looked after those who were valuable to him. I made myself valuable. I'd been behind the other students when I arrived, but I was hungry for the knowledge. I studied everything they threw at me, and then some. Everyone who went through the medical training program knew how to handle emergency care. Taylor's frequent expansion and conquests kept those skills in demand. But he also needed his soldiers in peak condition, and my side specialty was genetics.

The kind of genetics that made my much older brother look more like a thirty-year-old and gave him a fitness level closer to a man of nineteen.

The kind of genetics, at its simplest, that could cure Nora's baby.

I found myself walking past the bay Nora had been allocated. She was curled up in the chair facing the cot where her baby slept, eyes closed. She needed proper rest, but she refused to budge an inch from the cot. There was a world of hurt behind her pretty facade. Whether it was the medical profession, my age, or men in general, she had a deep-rooted aversion to, I couldn't say.

I wondered if the baby's father was still in the picture? If he was, I'd have thought he'd have been allowed to visit by now. And she hadn't mentioned anyone needing to know. There was a brand at her temple. I was tempted to check it against the database—it wasn't abusing my privilege; I was merely helping the processing team out.

Who the fuck was I trying to fool? I should back the hell away. An idiot could see she harbored the kind of damage that went soul-deep. Physically, she was healthy. Mentally, she was battling with depression that had been exasperated, I was sure, by her son's medical condition.

Everyone who survived the collapse had their share of mental trauma. It was part of life. In the old world, she might have seen a therapist to help her. In the new world, we picked ourselves up and moved on as best we could.

"You're staring at me," she mumbled, opening one eye a crack.

My lips tugged up in a smirk. *Guilty as charged.* With impressive self-control, I kept my focus on her face and not the rack that no amount of baggy clothing could hope to disguise. I thought she might be breastfeeding, but the report indicated that Adam was on solid food supplemented with formula.

So, her tits were just naturally big.

There was going to be a damn riot.

"You're not sleeping," I countered. "I was deciding whether I should give you a sedative. You're no use to your son if you drop from exhaustion." I pointed at the medical bed to her left that she had refused to use because it took her a few feet away from her baby. "If we can move his cot closer, will you try to rest?"

"Maybe." Both eyes were open, and she was studying the bed dubiously.

"You can try and rest the usual way, or I can get that sedative." I kept my tone professional—she did not do teasing well. "No one will touch you or Adam while you're here. I promise it's safe here."

I didn't mention what came after. If her owner lived, she would be reunited, and their new home would depend on how useful he was to Taylor's ever-expanding empire. If she didn't have an owner on our database, she would be allocated a new one. She was pretty, still young... and endowed with greater than average assets. Despite her mental issues and dependent child, there would be no shortage of willing petitions.

The soldier who'd brought her in had already sent me a message asking what her name was and whether she had an owner. Usually, I humored such requests with the information if I had it. This time, I'd told the nosey bastard to fuck off and follow the process.

"You're still staring," she said, her voice losing the abrasive edge, although her expressive eyes remained wary.

I tramped down the rage I felt toward the soldier who was only doing what dozens had done before—trying to gain an edge on the game. "You're still not on the bed, and I'm still deciding on the sedative. But I'm thinking if you're not there in the next ten seconds, I'll be making a call."

Her eyes widened. I could do brusque when I needed to. I was a doctor and used to dealing with all manner of insubordination from patients who were as often military as civilian.

"Ten..."

"The fuck," she mumbled, but she was getting up from the chair.

"Nine..."

"You said you'd bring his cot closer!"

"Eight... I'll sort that out once you've done as you're told."

She groaned and rolled her eyes.

"Seven..." I folded my arms.

"Six..."

Shooting a baleful look my way, she threw herself at the bed. "I'm here already! Please, bring him closer."

Biting back a smirk, I called a nurse over to help me move Adam's cot. Nora watched the process anxiously and didn't settle until he was close enough to touch.

As the nurse left, I felt her eyes on me. "I don't sleep well," she said. "Even when I was in Sanctuary. But I don't want a sedative."

"No sedative," I agreed. "I'm here on duty for the next four hours and will be passing back regularly during that time. I'll introduce you to the next doctor." My lips tugged up. "Doctor Nile is older than God and renowned for her lack of tolerance with patients who don't follow instructions. Get some rest."

She closed her eyes in a resolute way of someone faking sleep. When I checked back five minutes later, I was confident she was already asleep.

Chapter Eight

Blaine

As I headed for the fridge, I wondered what the hell I would do with Ava—not her real name, Ava—besides the obvious. And it was obvious I wasn't going to be going down that path any time soon, if at all.

I wasn't a man blessed with patience or compassion. The magnitude of having her here, and the responsibility she instilled, held an unexpected weight.

I should have known that anyone living in an environment as isolated as Sanctuary carried their share of personal baggage, which was exactly why I should have left well enough alone. Yet, having made the decision back on that rooftop, I felt compelled to continue.

Truth was, I was no more inclined to pass her off now than I had been at the start.

I was exhausted after seven grueling days on the most significant operation to date. Downtime didn't exist. Tomorrow, I'd need to assess any developments and work through the task of maintaining peace. Trouble would flare; it always did. By the time we achieved something nearing stability, Taylor would be eyeing his next prize, and we'd start the process once again.

She was still standing at the door. Fine, she could stay there all fucking night if that was what it took to convince her I wasn't about to throw her on the nearest flat surface and rape her.

Although why she was regarding me with terror was a mystery given she had chewed my ass out in the Humvee. I'd seen men slap women half-unconscious for less. Most women who spoke like that could generally give a punch as well as they could take it; Ava could do neither.

It was a lucky punch, I told myself with a smirk.

The fridge revealed several meals that could be quickly heated, left here courtesy of my housekeeper. None of them interested me.

What had I expected?

At first, I'd sought only to remove her from the danger of the streets. Maybe in the back of my mind, I'd pictured her falling gratefully into my bed. By the time the novelty of ownership had worn off, I'd have lined up another owner.

Now all I could hear was Carter's warning and see the fear in her eyes.

With hindsight, she was as ill-equipped for the world inside as she was for the one outside. There was, unfortunately, no quick or easy way to allay those fears. Atrocities of every kind had occurred since the collapse.

I picked up a chicken pot roast then shoved it back. What the fuck kind of food would she eat, anyway?

Within the communities, things were more controlled. Outside was another matter; the endless expanse that existed between the pockets of relative safety had been abandoned to the vultures. There, it was survival of the fittest in its most literal sense.

The thought of any woman being out there was bad enough, but someone like Ava would be in for a world of hurt. Some people only needed half an excuse, and there had been plenty of excuses.

"Pasta?" When she didn't answer, I glanced over my shoulder to make sure she wasn't lying in an unconscious heap by the door. She had moved further into the room to stare out of the window at the blackness beyond.

"You have pasta?"

"Yeah, I have someone come around, clean up. She stocks the fridge for me. I tend to be—" I decided not to elaborate. Going into the graphic details of my occupation wouldn't be helpful. "Busy."

"I love pasta," she stated with a tiny smile. It disappeared as quickly as it arrived, and she faked interest in the view from the window. Taking the dish, I shoved it in the microwave. A small sticky note on the top stated the required minutes.

It kicked off cooking with a whirr.

"My parents had an apartment in Manhattan," she said. "There were a lot more lights back then."

Her profile allowed me to observe her unawares.

She was so fucking beautiful. And damn if I wasn't thinking about going over there, pinning her against the window, and fucking her into next week.

"The war changed many things. Ready electricity was one of them," I said, grabbing a couple of plates from the cupboard. Carter said her genetic modifications were cutting edge. Her comment on her former life provided further enlightenment.

There was beer in the fridge but I went straight to the hard stuff. "You want a drink?"

When she shook her head, I poured myself a good measure of whiskey.

It had been a rough week. Next week wouldn't be much better.

I'd done enough reconnaissance in the newly claimed territory over the last few months to know it would be better for the people under Taylor's rule. But resistance was the norm, and it was wise to anticipate it.

Taking a good slug of the whiskey, I ran my fingers along my ribs. They were aching enough that they were possibly cracked. I should have gotten them checked at the hospital. I'd had other things on my mind at the time, and now my body was reminding me.

I poured another generous measure as the microwave gave its bong of completion.

Her eyes were on me as I dished out the food, and balancing the glass, I carried them over to the low seating area before the window.

"Thanks." She took the offered plate from me before sitting neatly on the end of the farthest seat.

Well, wasn't this fucking awkward.

I wasn't even hungry anymore. My ribs throbbed like a bastard. Had she not been here, I'd be drowning out the pain the liquid way. Knocking back another gulp of pain relief, I dumped the glass on the table and sat back on the couch.

I ate, shoveling it in efficiently because the quicker I finished it, the quicker I could lay down.

She took a tentative bite. "This is lovely."

I stared at the plate of food, but I was thinking about my mark at her temple. The brand of ownership was both fucked-up and primitively compelling. Couple that with my recent relationship with violence, and it was little wonder I was still thinking about fucking her, even as much pain as I was in.

Silence descended. I was glad she was eating and not trying to make small-talk. I managed half the plate before dumping it on the low table. My body was fucked. I knocked back the whiskey and wished I'd had the foresight to bring the bottle over. With a grunt, I lay on the soft couch, my eyes drifting shut.

"Are you okay?"

When I opened my eyes a crack, I found her leaning over me, brows drawn together in concern.

"Yeah, I cracked a rib, I think. It'll be fine tomorrow. I'm going to stay here for a bit."—All night —"Take the third door on the right when you're ready. It should be made up."

I closed them again, willing her to move out of reach.

"Blaine?"

No such luck. I opened my eyes fully to find her closer still. "Thank you." She left the room so fast that I wondered if I'd imagined it.

But exhaustion was pulling me under, and I had no choice but to submit to my body's demands.

Chapter Nine

Ava

It was the softest bed I could remember sleeping on, heaven. For a few blissful moments, I thought the end-of-days had been a bizarre dream. Believed I was in my parents' house, in my old bed and my old life.

My eyes snapped open to reveal the muted tones that were nothing like the soft lilac decor that had adorned my childhood bedroom.

Cold, hard, uncompromising reality crashed in, sending my heart into overdrive. It hammered furiously in my chest until the panic subsided enough for me to locate a sliver of rationale.

The door was still shut.

I was alone.

No terror was about to imminently assail me.

Tentatively, I drew the cover aside, feeling overly hot and crumpled, having slept fully clothed. Not that Blaine had looked capable of anything other than sleep. And nor had he done anything to suggest he was about to call on his ownership rights.

I'd spent enough time around soldiers to know that they often took themselves to the limits of human endurance. When they finally let go, they were pretty much unconscious as their body repaired. If his face was anything to go by, he'd needed the rest.

No sounds came from beyond the room. But I still rolled out the bed slowly and padded over to the door where I pressed my ear to it and listened.

Nothing.

Maybe he was still sleeping?

Investigating the tiny shower room, and seeing it had a lock, I decided to take a shower once I'd finished the necessities. The tiny bolt was designed during a bygone era when bathroom locks were about etiquette rather than protection from a futuristic war god.

He could probably put his shoulder to the door and spring it easily, but I still felt safer as I pushed that tiny bolt across.

Stripping out of my clothes, I stepped under the spray. It was warm and felt wonderful, but I was still a little unsteady. Jodi would throw a fit when she found out what I'd done.

Only Jodi would never know.

I didn't even know where she was or about anyone else in Sanctuary. I needed to ask him. I felt sick thinking about asking him anything. I damn near swallowed my tongue last night getting a few words out.

It was probably for the best after my earlier rant in the Humvee.

Everything was so... raw.

A dead space opened inside me, and I took a steadying breath, willing myself to maintain my composure in the face of the rising emotional storm. This time, I did better and got through the shower without breaking down. I put yesterday's clothes on for the lack of alternative, and returning to the bedroom, drew the curtains open.

Daylight greeted me. The clouds had lifted, casting weak dawn light over a starkly ravaged cityscape.

A shocked hiss escaped my lips. It had been years since I'd witnessed the destruction in such bold glory. During my three days on the streets, the light rain and endless grey skies had masked much of it. And the lack of windows within Sanctuary had shielded me from the reality of our world.

Today, the tragedy of all that had happened was a fresh wound.

What have we done?

A seemingly endless vista of skyscrapers stretched into the distance: derelict, whole, and every aspect in-between.

I missed Jodi; she had been something reliable and undemanding in a broken world. I allowed myself a precious moment to accept this, to explore the pain before I shut it away. Without Jodi, I would have gone crazy long since, and her absence left a hole that I'd no idea how to fill. Surviving without her would be difficult.

"There's nothing more final than death. Anything else is a bonus." Mary had made that phrase a kind of worship when people stopped worshipping a god. I would survive. Jodi would never give up, and I wouldn't either.

A light tap on my door snapped my head around.

He'd knocked. That had to mean something, right?

My heart thudded double time in my chest as I walked toward it and drew it open without hesitation.

He was dressed in black again. The T-shirt fitted snugly enough that I could see every contour of his insanely built body. The man had a presence that went beyond my life experiences.

Was he enhanced? Many of the soldiers were. Jodi had received a few of the basics before she became my bodyguard. Yesterday's bruising on his face had faded while his body had lost the stiffness I'd noticed last night.

"I need to leave," he said gruffly, running fingers through his hair in a way that suggested this was not to his liking.

The movement sent muscles rippling across his chest, which my eyes tracked subconsciously for several seconds until I realized what I was doing and snapped them away. Thankfully, he was distracted by something bleeping on his watch.

"You need to stay inside. I'll get back as soon as I can." His lips formed a line as he dragged his attention from the watch.

Our eyes met.

I swallowed.

Was he expecting me to bolt as soon as his back was turned? "I won't try to leave," I stated quickly, wondering if he would lock me in a room or, worse, tie me up if I didn't acknowledge his order.

It had been dark last night when we arrived, but I'd seen enough to know the building was a fortress. I had no desire to draw the attention of the security personnel patrolling the grounds.

"I'll need to lock you in," he said, eyes never wavering from mine. I thought he was talking about the room for a wild moment, but he gestured toward the front door. "It's security coded. If anyone but me tries to enter or leave, I'll receive a notification."

Lowering my eyes, I nodded. Blaine seemed impossibly larger in the light of day. It had been years since I'd been alone with a man other than the few who had joined Sanctuary. Jodi had always been there, fierce in her protectiveness. She had punched a guy once who paid me too much attention, and the next reconnaissance mission, he'd never come back.

I didn't ask her what had happened. Whether she had killed him or sent him on his way.

She had killed men for me before—when she needed to.

Today, I had no Jodi to protect me, yet the man standing before me still didn't feel like a threat.

I thought he should have. But some kind of weird cross-wiring was going on in my brain, and all I could think about was the way his T-shirt stretched over muscles.

I'd been with men. A long time ago now. But I did remember what they felt like over me, under me... inside me.

My memory whispered that those men weren't built like this. Either I had a poor memory, or Blaine was exceptional.

"There's plenty of food and stuff," he said, breaking the stretched silence. Then he turned and headed toward the door, snatching up his duster from where he'd left it crumpled over the couch the night before.

The door shut with a soft click.

In his absence, I let out a shaky breath. The tension had been palpable. He was gone, and in a way that suggested he would not be back for a while.

Time was a blessing that could be used to come to terms with what had transpired and accept that my life was presently out of my control.

I walked over to the lounge area and that vast expansive window where I stared with unseeing eyes into the distance.

Soon, I realized that time was, if anything, a curse allowing me to wallow in despair.

I sat on the couch and watched the clouds roll by.

I cried.

I wondered about my friends and about my future, and strangely although I hadn't done so for a very long time, I thought about my mother. And thought too, about that fateful day when the monster told me that she was dead. I'd gone to

Jodi afterward and spoke the words that my bodyguard—and dearest friend—had been longing to hear.

"Get me out of here, Jodi. As far away as we can go."

The monster hadn't been expecting me to act so quickly, had expected me to be broken and weak so that he might mold me to his whims. But we'd fled that same night. It was the best decision I'd ever made.

Blaine

"I hear you've finally embraced the path of corruption and claimed ownership?"

The question distracted me just as the apartment door burst open and all hell broke loose. I copped a punch to the face, the blow catching my cheekbone and sending me flying backward. I hit the corridor wall with a thud that further rattled my teeth. My glare promised a world of hurt on Mitch before I launched myself back into the fray.

"Great timing, asshole," I muttered. Getting a lock on a thug's neck, I beat his head into the wall.

The fucker was high. We wrestled. I kneed him in the face and smacked his head into the wall twice more before he dropped out cold. Weapons fire dissected shrill screams and rough cursing.

Fuck me, how many people were in the apartment?

Another group surged from a back room, bullets tearing into the wall beside me, sending a spray of concrete chips.

We ducked, returned fire. They retreated; we followed in.

More screams.

A chair came flying through a doorway. Mitch ducked the worst of it but caught a leg. A thug followed through, tackling

Mitch to the floor where they grappled amid thrashing legs and flying fists.

More weapons fire and screams followed before quiet descended, broken only by the muffled grunts and thrashing as Mitch fought with his new buddy.

"Get the fucker off me!"

Smirking at his overreaction, I waved the nearest soldier over, and he peeled the raging drug dealer off.

"Don't—" I was about to suggest we save one for questioning, but Mitch had already staggered to his feet and put a bullet through his head. "Kill him," I finished anyway.

Blood splattered the wall behind. Mitch grunted in disgust as he dropped the man to the floor. "You took your fucking time."

"Clear!" The call came from deeper inside the warren of rooms.

Ignoring Mitch, I stepped over the body and into the back room.

"Didn't realize you were going to be so sensitive about it," Mitch said, following behind me.

I glanced back, then chuckled.

"What?" Mitch demanded, eyes narrowing.

"You look a mess," I said. His teeth were coated in blood, and more trickled down his chin.

"I bit my tongue," he said, grimacing. "Stings like a bastard. Glad all my shots are up to date. I don't even want to think about what disease these lowlifes are carrying."

Dirty, tattered rags hung at the window that let grainy light spill over a chaotic mismatch of furniture and an assembly of low-grade drug processing paraphernalia. The low-rise complex was abandoned, but we'd heard a gang had set up here. As part of Taylor's post-takeover cleansing, he liked any known drug players dealt with.

I gave the signal to wrap it up. Feet shuffled and stomped as everyone but Mitch and I cleared out.

Mitch tapped his ear communicator. "Anything else to report in the sweep?" The negative confirmation came back. "Ok, we've got the processing area here. Clear the building ASAP."

Rummaging in his backpack, Mitch pulled out a small explosive pack. I raised a brow as he placed it in the middle of the nearest table. I was pretty sure a grenade would do the job. "So, who's the woman then? Carter said she came from the civilian enclave we took out?" He hefted the backpack over his shoulder and headed out the door.

"Carter has a big mouth," I replied, following Mitch down the stairs and through the ground floor complex before shoving out the big double entry doors and into the courtyard where the team had assembled. A quick count confirmed everyone was present, and Mitch hit the remote detonator.

An explosion tore through the building. Everyone instinctively ducked—except Mitch—as the entire first floor windows shattered, raining glass, splinters of wood and brick.

Mitch grunted and cast a glance over his shoulder at the broken building. "Must have been more chemicals in the room than I thought," he said distractedly.

"Nice job," someone quipped sarcastically—Mitch was renowned for his overzealous use of explosives.

Banter followed, but I was only half paying attention. I was thinking about the woman I now owned, alone in my apartment.

Chapter Ten

Ava

The day had been a personal roller coaster to hell and back. As the light faded, I was still alone.

I'd picked at some food, but without real appetite. While in Sanctuary, I occupied myself in the computer labs where I'd written and modified various control applications that governed everything from the defense turrets to the lighting and reticulation in the cultivation bays.

I'd acquired skills that were best described as 'hacking' while living with my uncle. It was the only reason Jodi and I had escaped. They found a better use in the community of Sanctuary. There was always something new to be added or updated.

The lack of purpose was only one problem here, isolation was the other. In Sanctuary, you were never alone. Fellow community members were always close, the few children running boisterously, and the surrounding industry that kept it all working. Everything had an order and purpose; no one sat idle.

In the post-apocalyptic world, thinking time was unhealthy, and here I was with an abundance of it.

Eventually, as the light faded, I lay on the huge couch and willed sleep to take me. I didn't sleep, but I napped, and when the sound of the door opening came, the event didn't penetrate the conscious part of my mind.

The arrival of Blaine at the side of the couch did.

Disorientated, I lurched to a seated position. The lighting remained dimmed, as I'd set it when laying down to rest. The clock revealed it was the early hours of the morning. Given he'd left at dawn, he'd been gone nearly twenty-four hours.

"You okay?" Frowning, he yanked off the duster. Like last time, he began to systematically remove and store weapons in the hidden panel, glancing back over his shoulder when I remained rooted to the couch, mute.

"I'm fine, thank you," I stammered, rising and wondering what I was supposed to do.

I wiped damp palms on my pants. The situation was surreal; I'd no point of reference as to how I should act. The laws of ownership were not unknown to me, and yet I'd been in Sanctuary for six long years. Before that, they hadn't applied in the usual sense since I'd been under the guardianship of someone powerful enough to see to my protection. As warped and unwelcome as that guardianship had been, it had allowed me to remain above the usual application of ownership.

As the panel slid smoothly shut, he turned back, revealing fresh bruising on his face. What had he been doing all day and half the night?

Perhaps sensing my unspoken question, he shrugged and said, "Just another day in the office."

I snorted out an involuntary laugh. I doubted he'd sustained that damage while in an office unless the office happened to be full of lawless outsiders, and he'd been standing between them and their favorite drug.

He didn't move. The tension stretched between us. He ought to be doing something, getting something to eat maybe, or telling me to get him something to eat. Anything but standing there staring at me with so much emotion, I felt it leaking into my pores.

That look. Damn, that look dripped with inevitability.

His chest rose as he drew a deep breath before letting it out slowly. "Come here."

Had he spoken, or had fear plucked the comment out of some dark terrorized recess of my mind?

"I'm not going to hurt you." His voice was still the gruff one that set flutters low in my belly. And his body language was impossible to interpret in the subdued lighting.

He was my owner. I had agreed to this, and as dubious as that consent was, I'd understood the consequence when I'd agreed.

He didn't repeat himself, and the silent command hung between us.

Willing myself to put one foot before the other, I fought an internal battle between common sense and the foolish desire for flight. Running would get me nowhere and more likely provoke him.

Despite this assessment's logic, my legs had a will of their own, and still, I didn't move.

He shifted so slightly that I might have missed it had I not been so hyper-aware. Relaxed, as though my internal struggle was of no consequence to him.

As though unconcerned by whichever outcome should prevail.

In direct contrast, my anxiety rose, pressure spiraling outward from my core.

It was Blaine who broke the impasse, approaching with slow, unhurried steps. He invaded that invisible sanctum of personal space, crowding me.

His scent washed over me, clean man, and a little smoke. Had he cleaned up somewhere before coming home?

I was reminded again of his size as he towered over me, trapping me between the wall of his body and the couch. My eyes found the center of his chest. He could break me, should he choose to, with disturbing ease. Heat radiating from his body, seeping into me.

He edged slightly closer, gentle as he drew my hair from one side of my face.

Surrounded.

My chest rose and fell steadily as he settled his fingers at the base of my throat, collaring me.

I blinked. Swallowed.

Head dipping, his lips brushed my cheek. He pulled back, studying me, gauging me, before dipping his head once more, this time to capture my lips.

Repeating this over and over, he seduced me one perfect kiss at a time. Each too brief press of his lips, and each retreat, coaxed me deeper into a dark, welcoming abyss. He wasn't going to hurt me; he had said so, and I believed him. At the same time, he would not allow my withdrawal.

The kisses became deeper, more urgent, as he pulled me into him, making me aware of our differences, of how much more powerful he was than I, of how little control of this situation I had. My free will abandoned me. I opened up to him and his kisses. I unraveled until I became a single thread that he commanded full control of. The stony plains of his body offered both safety and danger of the most sinful kind.

The instant I came to terms with his possession, he withdrew, leaving me dizzy and disorientated. Finding my fingers curled tightly into the material of his shirt, I released it, confused.

He sighed. "Go to bed, Ava." Stepping back, he offered space that I didn't want anymore.

What was I doing?

I fled to my room where I lay fully clothed upon the bed. My thoughts became a jumble. I convinced myself I had done wrong and worried about what his rejection meant. I didn't want him; I shouldn't want him. I should be biding my time until I could once more flee.

Despite the lateness, it took a long time before sleep took me, and when it did, it dragged me deep into darkly troubled dreams where past monsters hunted me.

Blaine

I drank too much whiskey and didn't eat any food. My enhanced body metabolized alcohol quickly, so it took a lot to get a buzz. All the while pacing my apartment like a caged beast. It had been weeks since I'd gotten laid. Not unusual during an operation, but the worst of it was over now.

My routine had gotten fucked up when I found a woman on that rooftop.

She was mine now. No one would give a fuck what happened to her within these walls. They didn't care much outside of them either, although Taylor liked to maintain a semi-civilized facade.

I didn't arrive into the world via a void. I had a mother and a father who had raised me to be a decent man. But that was many years ago. The time when women were treated like equals had been and gone. Now they were possessions.

Seventeen years didn't erase your memory, but it did dim it considerably. I found it hard to recall how I'd once been toward women when so much had happened since.

I wasn't the same man—too much ugly during that intervening period.

I'd had every experimental enhancement a human could handle and a few that produced questionable side effects. The death, the killing, the hardness of survival had also taken their toll.

Bringing my pacing to a stop, I tossed the empty bottle on the couch.

Why had I sent her to bed?

This time I didn't knock, and the door swung open, thudding against the inner wall. Ava shot up in bed, a squeal escaping her lips. Light spilled from the doorway behind me, casting weak illumination. Her chest heaved unsteadily—she was still dressed under the light cover—and her unnaturally pale eyes shone luminescent.

"You said you understood how this works?" I remained rooted in the doorway, gripped by an irrational rage.

"I do." Her voice was soft and a little breathless. She looked around like she was reminding herself where she was. "I've never been owned before. I don't know what to do." Her eyes met and held mine. "I don't know how I'm supposed to act."

Her words calmed my rage, some.

"I want it all," I said. "I want you in my bed. And I want you fucking willing. Or I will find you someone else. If you're staying in my home under my protection, then I will have my due."

"You sent me to bed." Her fingers clenched over the covers. "I'm—willing."

A gasp accompanied me scooping her up. Her legs wrapped around my waist in a way that felt like home.

Stalking along the corridor, I kicked my bedroom door open. Taking her down on my bed, I fisted a handful of her hair and closed my mouth over hers.

I felt unhinged. Maybe she sensed this and was seeking to pacify me. I didn't care so long as she didn't try to stop me because I wasn't sure I could.

True to her word, she was willing, open, and giving. My tongue met hers as a needy sob erupted from her chest. I ripped my mouth from hers, tugging impatiently at her T-shirt. "Off."

Her arms lifted so I could rip it over her head.

There I stopped, caging her body, eyes locked on her perfect plump tits. My hand shook a little as I palmed the side of her waist and skimmed slowly up until I enclosed the whole of one heavenly mound. She was so fucking tiny everywhere but here. So fucking soft and perfect. Even before the proverbial shit hit the fan, something this perfect wasn't for the likes of me.

Her breath stuttered, ragged gasps that turned to a moan as my thumb swept over the engorged tip.

"Oh god."

My eyes shot to hers. "You like that, baby?"

"Yes, god, yes."

I squeezed the tip before slowly rolling it. Her face contorted, mouth opening on a silent gasp, little ass wriggling against the bed. "Good because this is mine now, and I plan on enjoying what's mine." Leaning down, I circled the little nub with the tip of my tongue before drawing it into my mouth.

Soft.

Her little moans were setting my dick on fire. I squeezed her tit, sucking harder, drawing more into my greedy mouth.

When was the last time I'd done more than a quick, hard

fuck? I had vague recollections that it might have happened years ago—it was possible I'd dreamt it.

Lifting my head, I gave the other side the attention it deserved.

I was a rough man. Life had made me rough. Against her unblemished flesh, my hands looked obscene, big and coarse, and better suited to killing than touching the angel spread out for my pleasure on the bed. She was mine now. I was going to put my hands on her any way I wanted.

Impatient hands tugged at my T-shirt. I left off marking up her tits long enough to rip it over my head.

"God, please!"

Her impatience drove an echo in me. My teeth grazed the gentle swell of her belly as I popped the button on her cargo pants. They were far too big—I'd get her clothing tomorrow—they slipped off with ease, her panties following after.

"Fuck." I toed my boots off, fingers at my buckle. Still a little dizzy from the booze I'd downed and damn near embarrassing myself with how much I wanted inside.

"Open your legs, baby." I couldn't tear my eyes away from that hairless pussy as I stripped the last of my clothes. I could smell her fucking arousal. "Let me see how ready you are."

The briefest hesitation showed before she let her legs fall apart.

Finally, my pants came free and I kicked them to the floor, fisting my cock to ease the growing ache. One hand braced to the bed at her hip, I pumped slowly. "Wider, baby. Get your fingers on your pussy and hold yourself open for me."

Her chest heaved; I was sure she was about to balk. Then she slid those delicate little fingers down and parted her lips.

"You look wet, Ava. All slick and glistening." Fuck, I didn't trust myself to touch her and not fall on her like a savage. Her little hole was all pink and tight. "Are you wet and ready for my cock?"

"I—yes." Those impossibly colored eyes held mine. "It's been a long time. Please, don't hurt me."

I growled. A full, back-of-the-throat growl like I was a fucking beast. "Baby, my cock is about to fill your perfect little pussy all up, and I don't have gentle in me. Try and relax for me. Let me have you how I need to. It'll go easier if you do. But either way, I'm not going to stop. Now, get your fingers in there, baby, so I can see how tight you are."

Another sob, but the fingers of her right hand slipped down, and two disappeared inside.

"Good girl. Fuck that hot little pussy with them." I let off my cock before I came all over the bed, my hands skimming up her thighs as I watched her finger herself. When my right hand closed over hers, she went to pull away. "Ah-ah. Keep them nice and deep." Curling around her hand, I pressed my middle finger beside hers, slowly easing into that hot, wet, silken sheath. My other hand collared her throat as I leaned in to take her soft, sweet lips.

She twitched, thighs squeezing mine, trying to pull her hand away even as her pussy pulsed around our fingers.

I nipped at her bottom lip, and, trapping her hand within mine, rocked our fingers from side to side. Soon, wet squelching noises brought a flush to her pretty cheeks as she squirmed underneath me.

Ava

Nothing in my life had prepared me for Blaine and the pleasure he wrested from my body. I tasted whiskey on his lips, my nose full of his clean, masculine scent. The alcohol should have frightened me, but all it did was make me feel a little wild.

My fingers were trapped inside my pussy, his larger hand surrounding mine. My other hand curled against a shoulder that seemed impossibly wide.

Blaine's presence swamped my awareness, the size of his body, the strength evidenced in the dips and ridges of arms, chest, and abs, and his warning, as if I needed it, that he would claim his ownership rights.

Men were stronger than women. I doubted any woman who came through the collapse was ignorant to this fact. Jodi was the toughest woman I knew, but she was the exception, not the norm.

After we fled our former home, I'd pushed myself to the limits of my physique and had learned how to fight.

But as I lay under Blaine, I understood my weakness.

I understood my vulnerability.

He wasn't going to stop. It didn't matter what I said, nor whether I struggled or begged. My lack of control in this situation manifested an unexpected heightening of my arousal. I was so wet, and the obscene sounds seemed to make me twice as wet.

Our combined fingers were rocked from side to side, catching that sensitive bundle deep inside. Something was building, a terrible pressure that didn't feel quite right, making me fidget under his skilled ministrations.

"Keep fucking still," he growled, fingers tightening on my throat.

"I can't. I don't like it." I felt like I was going to... pee myself, and despite being absolutely convinced angering him would be a bad idea, acute embarrassment made me fight in earnest.

"Don't like it?" He increased the movement making me

squirm in earnest. "That wet sound is making my dick stone hard. You sure you don't like it?"

Everything was twisting up. I wanted to come. I was going to come, but there was also a terrible alien pressure. My struggles brought out his dominance. The more I fought, the more determined he became to pin me to the bed and torment me silly.

Somehow I managed to wrest my fingers out, but he replaced my smaller ones with three of his own.

"God! Please stop. I can't—"

His thumb swiped over my swollen clit, and I came in a heady rush, a gush flooding between my legs that was both intensely pleasurable and shocking. Heat swept over my body; my face felt like it was on fire.

"Fuck, that was hot," he growled before taking my lips in a drugging kiss. "I need inside you."

I blinked trying to work out where I was and what the hell I was doing. The bed was soaked underneath me, my breath unsteady, and my body, which should have been sated, hummed with anticipation.

He fumbled in the nightstand drawer, pulling out a tube. I tried not to look at the monster he was slicking up, but my eyes still gravitated there—thick, ruddy, with a thicker bell head.

I drew in a sharp breath. Yeah, that wasn't going to fit.

Tossing the tube aside, he cupped my cheek and brought my focus to his face. "You're tight, baby. How long since you had someone inside you?"

"I don't know—several years." They were not in the same league as Blaine, and I fought the rising tide of panic.

"Fucking tragedy," he said. "This perfection should be made to feel pleasure often." Then he nudged the entrance before sinking the tip slowly inside.

I squirmed, feeling my pussy pulse around the invasion.

I'd experienced pleasure, just not the kind derived via a cock for a long time. I determined correcting him was not in my best interests while I was vulnerable beneath him.

His lips lowered to my throat, gently nipping the flesh between teeth and bringing a full body shiver. My pussy clenched painfully over the tip of his cock. It jerked inside me as he trailed kisses over my throat, and up to the shell of my ear as he sank in another inch.

My pussy fluttered, confused between seeking more of the enticing fullness, and trying to push him out.

"Relax for me, Ava." He nuzzled the side of my throat, sucking more kisses against the skin. Between the lube and my slick pussy, he sank deeper with an ease that my straining channel did not like.

I tried to relax, but worry mounted, and my pussy locked down tight.

His lips closed over mine, tongue surging in time with the shallow surge and retreat of his cock. Hands roamed everywhere, gliding over my hip, waist, the side of my breast, before lowering again and drawing one knee up and out. He repeated on the other side while I crashed into full-blown panic. With me nearly in two, he thrust deep and stopped.

"God, please!" I planted my palms against his chest and pushed. There was too much of him, my straining muscles quivering to hold open.

"Almost there." The next thrust and his crotch came flush to mine. "Breathe, baby." His big hand closed over mine, easing them from his chest. My arms were shaking with the strain of pushing him away, and as soon as he removed them, his cock nudged in another fraction.

He brought my palm against the side of his throat, drawing my focus back to his face, the wild thud of his heart under the pulse point at his throat, and the rough stubble on his jaw.

"Oh god." My climax hit me out of nowhere. His impossible girth, the totality of his invasion, his scent, and those deep rumbly words were like a potent drug coursing through my veins. I bit my lip, trying to stifle my wild moan.

"So. Fucking. Tight." Kneeling up, he took my hips in his big hands and drew back, and slammed all the way back in. "Loosen up, babe."

My mind and body had no idea what to make of this. The heavy thrusts, the slapping of meeting flesh, and the stimulation against my swollen clit. I'd hit a climatic summit, and there was no way back down. He took his pleasure roughly, and I was merely along for the ride.

The visual of his powerful body was a source of stimulation all on its own, lean, corded muscles, the flash of white scarring scattered across his torso, the black tattoos over his shoulders across his pecs, and skimming the right side of his throat. At his temple was the same tattoo used to brand me. The mark of ownership binding us both together held an unexpected beauty. I belonged to him, this man who was as a god in a mortal world, and I, the helpless human he slaked his lusts upon.

As was inevitable, my inner muscles gave under the fierce coupling, and all the while, I pitched into a perpetual free fall. He braced over me, palming my ass so he could pound into me. Burying his face in the crook of my throat, he sucked. My stomach and pussy clenched, sending us both over the cliff.

My throat and pussy throbbed in tandem while his chest heaved against mine. And inside, I felt the hot flood and the rush of adrenaline as he filled me with cum.

I breathed, tried to work out what had just happened, and gave up.

He was half crushing me, yet my hands still roamed his shoulders and back, delighting in the feel of firm flesh and the closeness. It had been so long since I'd felt a man inside me, and the completeness brought an unexpected tightness to my chest.

My breath stuttered, preceding a guttural sob.

It was for the best that I'd enjoyed it, and no more a betrayal of my best friend than if I'd hated it.

But it felt a lot like betrayal, and hot tears spilled.

He pitched to the side, taking me with him, cock still inside me, still partially hard. Our combined cum, and the shaming evidence of pleasure, spilled out, turning the tops of my thighs slippery and further soaking the bedding. He didn't ask me what was wrong, and I was grateful for that.

How could I even explain when the whole world was wrong? I told myself I was only doing what I needed to survive, but the tears still fell.

Dreamless sleep took me, but only for a short time. It was still dark beyond the window when Blaine roused me, rolling above me and sliding between my parted thighs in a way that reeked of familiar. I hissed a little as he entered, sore muscles protesting at the penetration.

He took my lips as he took my body, cupping my cheek in his warm palm, hips moving in that time old rhythm. I rose with him. My body welcomed the stretch, the peace, the completion when he filled me, and the sense of bereft with each withdrawal. We were new to each other, yet our bodies found a connection that transcended words. I opened myself to him, let my legs lift to cradle his body, let my hands explore his back and ass, my hips rocking in tandem to his. Urgency replaced the languid sensuality, movements losing grace and gaining aggression. Heat rose, the rush of adrenaline as his body lifted to peak, triggering my climax.

Chests heaving in the aftermath, we shared breath as we stared at one another through the grey light of dawn.

"I need to leave," he said, glancing at his watch. Rolling off me, he strode toward the adjoining bathroom. The sounds of rushing water followed.

When he returned, he dressed efficiently. Muttered something about new clothes and headed for the door.

For the second time, I realized I'd failed to ask him about my friends.

Chapter Eleven

Carter

When I arrived for my next shift early, I convinced myself I was just being diligent.

This delusion lasted the entire journey from my apartment to the medical facility, up the elevator, and even to the nurse's station.

She wasn't here.

Moved on to the allocations team, who would assess her for usefulness. I wondered if she had any skills Taylor could use? If she did, it might go easier for her.

I smirked as I picked up the datapad and went through my round. Something told me she was going to kick up a storm.

Then my amusement faded because she was already a little broken, and I didn't like the thought of her being broken some more.

Taylor didn't tolerate dissension. Women without skills were allocated to an owner. Women with skills were still assigned an owner, but they got some choice. The dictator's plans all revolved around control and reward. The more useful you were, the more rewards you got, while those less useful were offered up to keep their betters sweet.

Blaine had told me that things were different before the collapse. I'd been a young boy at the time and barely remembered my parents, never mind how they'd acted toward one another. But I'd witnessed rape and abuse of every kind in the years before we arrived in Taylor's world. A woman would always be smaller and weaker than a man. It made sense that they should have the protection of an owner. A few were tough enough to hold their own, but they were few... and invariably had it rough in other ways.

Blaine said it was fucked up, which had always held me back from ownership. I'd been asked, though, a lot.

And now Blaine had claimed ownership, and I couldn't figure out how I felt about it.

It wasn't like owning someone was easy. It was a fickle world, and challenges were accepted as the norm. Each new batch of arrivals had a two year probation period before they were allowed to petition for the new women entering... or to challenge if they liked someone already taken.

The pretty ones changed hands a lot. The ones with enormous fucking tits changed hands even more.

She would be better off with a soldier.

Who was I kidding? I could take the guy who'd brought her in if it came down to it. I still trained with Blaine any chance we got, and he never went easy on me. I kept fit. You never knew when the delicate balance was going to tip us back into anarchy, and it paid to be prepared.

So yeah, I could offer a credible level of protection.

The day passed. An incident happened in the southern district and I was diverted to the emergency ward. I forgot all about a pretty redhead with a fiery attitude while I was wading through the blood.

Finally, we'd dealt with the most pressing emergencies, and a new shift arrived to relieve us.

I was tired, hungry, and a little cranky when I got a call from allocations.

Nora

"Doctor Carter!" The prissy allocation woman nearly tripped over her own feet, blushing furiously as the floppy-haired doctor was shown into the room. "I'm so sorry to have interrupted you for this. But the rules state we must follow up on ownership requests, no matter how unfeasible they may be." The look she sent my way was downright nasty, and I hugged Adam to my chest.

It had all gone downhill from the moment I'd left the medical facility, and it hadn't been great before. Herded onto a coach and taken to an austere concrete box of a building for allocation and processing. Shuffled from one room to the next with an ever-increasing set of papers neatly contained in a file. I'd been physically and mentally poked and prodded for what felt like hours: questions, tests, interviews.

Did I have any skills? One crusty old dude actually asked me this.

Really? I'd been fifteen when the collapse happened. I hadn't even finished high school, and I'd been average intelligence at best. After, I stumbled from one nightmare to the next. You didn't talk about the world before the collapse, that was the rule, but I didn't talk about life before Sanctuary, either.

Surviving was the only skill that mattered.

It was the only skill I had.

"No problem, Mandy," Carter replied, resting his hand on her shoulder in a way that was too familiar for my liking.

Huh? What the hell did I care about how familiar they were? Only I did care because an hour ago, I'd boldly announced that Doctor Carter had offered ownership rights for me.

I was officially on the crazy train and chugging off into loopy land.

"If you could give me a few minutes alone with Nora, that would be great." His tone was light and even, and yet somehow assertive. Without missing a beat, he guided Mandy, aka allocations bitch, over to the door.

"She wants to leave," Mandy continued. "I explained that her baby's procedure was expensive. A minimum of ten years is required for that level of debt. *Then* she suddenly decided you had offered ownership." She shook her head. "And James is sitting right outside, willing to take on mother, baby, and the debt. I'm so sorry to have even bothered you."

Carter shut the door while she was still talking.

My breath caught as I watched the tense lines of Carter's back as he stared at the closed door. Adam fussed, and I bounced him a little, grateful when he settled again. The pants and shirt I'd seen Carter wear at the medical center were swapped for jeans and a faded blue T-shirt that stretched across defined muscles.

Doctor Carter was built.

I tried to recall the man who'd seemed so non-threatening, but all I could see was his power.

He could hurt me so easily.

"What are you doing, Nora?" he asked. Turning slowly, he shoved hands in his jean's pockets and leaned back against the door. His hair was a little disheveled; he looked tired.

"I—" Yes, what was I doing? I swallowed. If it wasn't for that familiar voice, I might have thought him a different man. "I want to leave Guilder City."

His face scrunched. "Not happening, babe."

The endearment was unexpected and jarring. "I thought maybe you could talk to them..." I trailed off. There had been more that I'd intended to say about how I was no use to anyone as a pet, about how I could work in some other way to pay off the debt.

His eyes held mine, tic thumping in his jaw—he looked pissed.

Well, fuck him. No one was suggesting he debase himself because the world was full of shit.

"Hoping I had some sway?" His lips thinned. "You can forget it. Sure, I could pay off your debt if I was inclined to. But how's that going to work, hmm? To be blunt, you're barely keeping it together."

That was cutting and closer to the truth than I wanted to admit.

"You have someone waiting for you outside?"

Blinking a few times, I shook my head.

He huffed out a breath. "You can't care for Adam outside, not on your own," he continued with his damning assessment. "You'd be picked off within hours, days at the best. You know what they do to other men's babies outside?"

My throat turned to dust, and my tongue stuck to the roof of my mouth.

"They kill them, Nora. Maybe before they rape you, maybe after. Maybe at the same time." He spoke with the same even tone, but his eyes, they held all the fury. "So no, don't ask me to help you kill the boy I cured yesterday. Don't ask me to help you get raped, beaten, and likely killed, too. You called me here because you said you needed an owner. You already have one man willing to take on you and your baby. He'll be docked the administration fees for taking you straight from processing. The assholes and bullies who like to beat on women don't usually go to that kind of trouble. They just wait until the grace period is over and claim ownership the other way."

I didn't speak; I couldn't. Words were defeated by the lock terror had on my body.

His grunt held a note of derision, and leaning up from the door, he turned to leave.

"Please, don't."

His hand was on the handle. Resting there, poised to exit the room and my life.

"I don't know how to be owned." Fuck, this was difficult. The mark at my temple was hell, not ownership. I felt sick to my core. I was so tired it felt like forever since I'd had a decent night's sleep. My lips trembled—I would not cry. "I don't know James."

"You don't know me either." He took his fingers from the handle and turned back to face me. "And so we're clear, I don't know how to be an owner. I guess that evens things out. Is this you asking me to be your owner, Nora?"

Was I? I chewed on my bottom lip and almost prayed for Adam to fuss. Carter was right. I wouldn't last five minutes outside; I wasn't going to take my baby into that. And yet, I didn't have a clue how to be owned. Mandy, the allocations bitch, had been going over the details of all the damn rules when I'd had a full-blown panic attack and demanded to speak to someone from Sanctuary.

A probation period must be passed before I could speak to anyone, I was told.

Finally, out of desperation, I'd asked for Doctor Carter.

I was surprised they'd humored me.

I was even more surprised that he turned up.

"Nora, I'm going to need an answer."

I shrugged.

"That's not an answer, babe," he said softly.

I sucked in a breath, feeling my stomach tie in knots.

"Yes."

His lips tugged up on one side before he snatched open the door. "James." I heard the other man's acknowledgment before Carter continued, "Fuck off. Mandy, you can come back in."

The prissy allocations person returned as I was still gaping. The paperwork was completed with a pinched expression on her face. Then she said we were formally allocated and should proceed to branding.

"No need," Carter said. Pulling a chain from around his neck, he revealed a brander.

I'd only seen a few. Not every community had one. Some still used the old-fashioned technique using a needle and ink.

I'd hated the mark at my temple for so long, hadn't looked at myself in a mirror since the day the bastard had his men hold me down while he worked the crude tattoo into my flesh.

Expression intense, Carter lifted his hair to reveal an intricate tattoo. The brander beeped as he passed it over it, confirming it had locked in.

The allocations witch was forgotten as he tipped my chin. Gentle fingers brushed my hair from my forehead, a slight grimace as he noticed the rough tattoo. Then he passed the brander over me, and I was enrapt by the expression on his face, the way his eyes darkened, the way he brushed his thumb over it once it was done.

I'd thought Carter was the safe option, but as I met his steady gaze, all I saw was primal ownership.

What had I just done?

Chapter Twelve

Carter

Nora was silent for the journey to my apartment. It was late; the streets outside the car still glistened from rain earlier in the day. Adam cried on and off; he was due for his dinner soon, Nora had said. I'd asked her if she wanted to feed him before we left allocations, but she was keen to go and said the baby could wait for the short drive.

I couldn't blame her. I still remembered going through the same process when Blaine and I arrived. It had been a rough field canopy tent at the time, sectioned off for the various assessments. It had improved some over the years, but it was still a stressful time.

Adam began crying in earnest. I had a feeling he might degenerate into full-blown wailing at any point. They'd given us a pack of essential supplies, including a fold-out crib. He was going to need more stuff imminently.

What did I know about babies? I didn't even know anyone who had kids of any age. I went from the hospital to my apartment and didn't do a lot between. Blaine had an apartment in the same building—a little higher up and three times the size, not that I was complaining. If he was around, I'd spend some time with him in the evening, and we trained together a couple of times a week when our shifts permitted.

Not much chance of that happening given he'd just taken ownership of Ava. And it was always hectic for him immediately after Taylor claimed a new territory. This was the single largest expansion the self-appointed king had taken. I expected both of us to be busy for a while.

As we entered my home, the dam burst and the kid emitted a scream loud enough to wake the dead.

"I'm sorry," Nora said.

I winced and swiped a hand down my face. His screaming reached a new crescendo as she lay him on the rug to check his diaper.

Diapers... what the fuck did I know about diapers?

Absolutely nothing.

My apartment was open-plan; there was nowhere to go other than the bedroom. I made myself busy in the kitchen area... doing nothing... this was initiation by fire.

When I lifted my head, she had finished and was rummaging in the bag. Meanwhile, Adam continued to scream, kicking his small arms and legs, and face contorted in rage.

"Do you need help?" Despite my determination that I was useless, I was willing to try anything to make the ear-splitting sounds stop.

"I'm fine." The bag tipped over sending the contents spilling over the wooden floor. Packets, boxes, and clothing slipped and scattered, a couple of canisters rolled all the way under the couch.

"For fuck's sake," I muttered.

She cut me a glare over her shoulder. "Have you any experience with a baby? Have you ever held one before?"

I scowled. "Of course I've held a baby. I am a doctor, and they do cross my path from time to time." I was sort of telling the truth. Usually, I got a nurse to deal with the non-medical side of things.

As if sensing the growing animosity between his mother and me, Adam cranked it up another decibel.

"Fine then," she said. "Hold him."

Still on her knees, she collected Adam—now red of face and thrashing about like something possessed—and handed him off to me.

I'm not sure who was more shocked by this development, Adam or me. But as I hoisted him up to eye level, the cries petered out and he blinked at me through red-rimmed eyes. He hiccupped—it was super cute and brought a smile to my face.

"So, you have a civilized side, hmm?" A small, chubby fist beat the side of my head just to nip that delusion in the bud. "Uff, nice right hook, buddy. Your momma teach you that?"

When I glanced back at Nora, she was kneeling beside the bag, biting her lip to stifle a smile. Her face had softened, transforming pretty into stunning. "He needs to work on his manners," she said quietly.

Adam stopped beating me and began gouging his surprisingly sharp little nails into my cheek. I gently removed the offending hand.

"He's never been held by a man before." She turned away, stuffing the scattered supplies back into the bag.

That was pretty fucked-up.

"Leave it," I said. "You said he was hungry. I'll pick it up in a bit."

She nodded, grabbing a food pack. "Do you have a bowl and a spoon?"

I thumbed in the direction of the kitchen, and she went to find what she needed.

Shattered after the double shift in the emergency ward, I wanted desperately to sit down, but I was terrified to move in case Adam started wailing again.

He had Nora's eyes, I realized, big, electric blue eyes that stared at me with a disconcerting level of interest. The small arms flapped without coordination before his tiny fist made a grab for my cheek again. "Ah, ah buddy, I like my skin attached." His little jaw worked as he babbled nonsense.

Food prepared, Nora returned to collect Adam from me. There was something weirdly intimate about passing a baby between us. She took the couch; I took the easy chair opposite. Mentally bracing for more trouble, I was surprised when he ate his food like a champ and promptly fell asleep, head against her chest.

Yes, I was now staring at her chest not for the first time, but I had a valid excuse, right? I tried not to think about how big her tits might get if she was breastfeeding, but the imagery assaulted me nonetheless.

Silence followed.

A mess was scattered all over the floor. I should pick it up, but Adam was sleeping, and I didn't want to wake him up.

The magnitude of what I'd agreed to hit. My apartment wasn't large. I had two bedrooms; the second was currently being used as an office. My furnishings were nice—it came like this when Taylor handed me the keys a few years ago. Short of something breaking down, you took what you were offered and made no complaints.

But it wasn't kid-friendly. Not by a long shot.

"You want something to eat?"

She shook her head, not meeting my eyes.

What the hell was I doing? I should have let her go to James.

"Yeah, I'm not hungry, either." I glanced at my watch and grimaced when I saw what the time was.

"You look tired," she said. I wasn't sure what to do with this less abrasive version of her. "They said I could do some support work. There were a few options—one was at the hospital."

"Yeah, I saw it. But you'll get a few days' grace. Didn't Mandy explain that to you?"

Her lips thinned at the mention of Mandy. Yeah, that had been super uncomfortable, too. I mean, what were the chances?

Nora

"Have you slept with her?"

Why would I even ask that?

"What? Who?" he muttered, frowning.

Seriously, I was starting to get a feel for the way this community worked. It was clear ownership was a loose construct in which owned women were bartered like favors. I had come to the conclusion that many of them bartered themselves. "Allocations witch, Mandy."

Yes, I was going there.

He huffed out a breath. "Babe, it's been a long day. I double-shifted at the ER after some trouble kicked off. You asked me to be your owner. Have I fucked Mandy? No. Have I fucked her sister who works at the hospital? Yes. Not much I can do about that now is there. At the time when I was inside her, I wasn't planning on this."

Both the censure in his tone and the blunt words landed like a blow to the gut. He made a sweeping motion that encompassed me, Adam, and the carnage that covered the floor after I'd knocked over the bag. I felt a little sick and clammy. Judgment rights were not mine, and what was there even to judge?

My anger faded. I didn't know what I was angry about. I was tired, too. We were all tired; even Adam was out for the count. He was a good baby for the most part. I would miss Rachel looking out for him. I thought Rachel would miss Adam too. And now, I had to wait a full month before I could find out about anyone from Sanctuary.

"There's one bed," Carter said, stirring me from my rumination. "I'll talk to facilities about getting what you need for Adam tomorrow."

Standing, he headed through a door, which I presumed was his bedroom. I couldn't blame him for abandoning me. I was blunt at times, and he'd been even-tempered and supremely reasonable. I deserved to sleep out here on the couch.

I pressed a kiss to Adam's silky hair. The people and community who'd become dear to me had been snatched away. Carter was my owner now. At some point, he'd expect me to be more than a pain in his ass. I needed to get a grip. If I didn't, the floppy-haired doctor, who was nowhere near as unassuming as I'd first thought, would pass me off to someone else.

I had a baby. Adam might be quiet now, but he could scream when he had a mind to, and short of Rachel's miraculous skills, things didn't always soothe him.

Careful not to wake him, I settled Adam on the couch, and folded out the crib before laying him carefully inside. It wasn't great, but at least it allowed him to sleep safely.

My eyes shifted to the bedroom door. What was Doctor Carter thinking now that the reality of his agreement had manifested in all its messy glory? I hadn't expected him to come to allocations, never mind take responsibility for me as my owner.

Was he regretting that decision? Did he even realize the

kind of carnage a baby would bring to his life? The apartment was five times the size of the room I'd had at Sanctuary. It was like stepping into a pre-war magazine. Adam was starting to get around with surprising speed. He could haul himself up furniture, and his grabby little hands could find weak spots you didn't know existed. It was only a matter of time before he started walking, and that would be a whole other game.

Our position here was delicate enough without me running off my mouth.

I was busy berating myself when Carter returned. He'd changed into a pair of sleep pants that hung low on his hips.

My mouth turned to dust. No wonder Mandy was acting like a cat in heat. I still thought him too young and had expected him to be smooth. The smattering of hair seemed to accentuate the dips and ridges of muscle over his chest and abs. Scars marred his flesh, white, puckered knots and raised, jagged lines that told a story.

A heaviness settled behind my eyes, and I blinked back tears.

His masculinity and the violence evidenced on his body should have terrified me, but for reasons my tired mind could not understand, they only made him more real.

The eyes that held mine were shockingly vulnerable. "Most of it happened when I was a boy. Before my brother found me. The scars grew with me—they look worse than they are." He handed me a T-shirt. "If you want to change. The bathroom is right next to the bedroom. I'll carry his crib in. Come through when you've done."

"I can sleep here." The couch was softer than the bed I'd had back at Sanctuary. Sleeping on it wouldn't be a hardship, although it wasn't quite long enough. Over the years, I'd slept on a lot worse.

"Not happening," he said, tone brokering no argument. "I

let you sleep on the couch tonight, you'll want to sleep on the couch tomorrow. And before we know it, you'll be sleeping there all the time. You sleep in my bed."

My stomach dipped. He was right, damn it. We both knew he was right.

"There's a lock on the bathroom door. Don't make me take that privilege away. You have five minutes before I expect you to join me."

With those final words, he collected the crib and carried it and Adam into the bedroom.

Chapter Thirteen

Ava

Once Blaine left, I gathered up my scattered clothes and returned to my room to clean myself up.

I understood that he was expecting me in his bed from now on, but for reasons my tired brain couldn't unpick, sharing his shower felt like a step too far.

Having showered, I stared without joy at the dirty clothes I'd worn for two straight days.

I spent a few minutes wrestling with indecision. If today was anything like yesterday, he'd be gone for many hours. He'd mentioned something about getting clothes for me while he was unwrapping me last night. I could manage another day—I'd managed three days on the streets.

But I didn't put them on and instead returned to his room.

Taking a deep breath, I opened the closet door. My rummaging uncovered a pair of boxer-briefs and a T-shirt that were soft and clean. I'd shirked at using Blaine's shower, and now here I was slipping into his underwear.

A place this fancy had to have a washer. With luck, I could wash my clothes and have them back on before he knew. His closet was palatial, I'd never seen one person harbor so many clothes, and I doubted he'd miss what I'd taken.

Ignoring how intimate it felt having his clothes around me, I went in search of a laundry.

I found a state of the art washer and dryer that looked barely used. I was thrown back to the time before the collapse when such equipment was commonplace. At Sanctuary, we'd had a couple of old top-loaders that had been pilfered along the way. They were simple technology and easy to repair when parts broke down, as they invariably did over time.

Putting my clothes inside and hitting the button... and seeing it fill with water and start to wash, was an unexpectedly surreal experience.

Who was this man?

When he'd picked me up on the rooftop, I'd assumed he was a soldier. I still thought he was a soldier, but I also thought he was something more.

As I stared at the churning washer, my hands trembled. I tried to squash the memory of him rolling above me, the sweet ache as his cock filled me deep inside. My stomach turned over, and I drew a ragged breath.

I was still sore and tender; I wasn't used to having a man there and was confident he was packing more than average below the belt. The fact he'd had lube ready said he anticipated needing a little help. It brought unexpected questions as to my place here with him.

Clearly, I wasn't the only person he'd been intimate with in that bed.

I headed back to the lounge area as fresh worries hit me. An owner didn't need to explain himself. Didn't need to be monogamous before, after, or during the time he was an owner. I could feel the stickiness from where his cum lingered despite my best attempts to clean my sore pussy up.

He hadn't used a condom.

I wasn't on birth control.

I told myself that anyone who'd been clearly enhanced—and further was important enough to live in this home—wouldn't have a disease. He might even have had the birth control implant.

He might also want to get me pregnant.

I rubbed at my temples—just another thing to worry about like there wasn't already a queue.

On top of all this was the simmering guilt that I hadn't hated any of it.

I needed to focus.

I needed to not make this more complicated than it was.

He was my owner now. One day at a time, that was as far as I should think.

The views from the lounge window reminded me that I was in a new prison. I rarely thought about my old life and my parents. But my new situation had stirred memories up. My mother, and that monster I could not bear to call a relative even though he was.

I needed a distraction.

Yesterday, I'd taken care not to touch anything. Given his comments about the security alerts on the door and the sophisticated weapons storage, there might be other security within the apartment, perhaps even cameras.

The day passed slowly. I occupied myself by tidying up and making the beds.

An empty whiskey bottle lay on the couch, which explained the alcohol I'd smelled on him last night. It was mundane, but it was something to do. The place had looked super clean when I arrived... was it only two days ago? He'd mentioned someone coming around and stocking the food—I wasn't sure I was ready to meet someone new yet.

An old electric reader rested on the coffee table, but it contained only books on military strategy. Pertinent given the environment we lived in, but not conducive to distraction.

The washer finished, and I put my clothes in the dryer.

My thoughts could not be contained; they drifted relentlessly back to the people of Sanctuary. I didn't want to think about what I had shared with Blaine, it took center stage nevertheless.

I wondered where he was and what he was doing.

Whether he would return, bruised and battered.

Whether he would take me straight to bed.

These troubled thoughts led to cycles of despair. I was a leaf floating on a river subject to currents beyond my control.

Alone.

Isolated.

Would I go insane in my new luxury confinement?

My boredom gave way to an idle investigation of my surroundings. The main living space was functional but cold; nothing here could be implied to be personal in any way. I found an office of sorts with a small desk and a computer. It was off, and I wasn't brave enough to try switching it on.

My rambling returned me to his bedroom. Earlier, I'd opened the heavy drapes to reveal the depressive cityscape. Smoke rose in the distance from several sources, and as I watched, another plume made its debut.

Fresh troubles were brewing down there.

Another datapad rested on the nightstand. This one was print protected, which immediately piqued my interest. It was possible to get around it, not easy certainly, but possible with enough patience and time.

Something I had in abundance.

The last time I'd resorted to such underhand work was when a Sanctuary member took off. He'd left behind a computer. Jodi had ordered me to hack it. I managed it after a few days—my teenage years had yielded some interesting skills.

A faint click from the direction of the front door sent a flood of adrenaline rushing. I fumbled the device, my hasty attempt to return it to the table failing as it clattered to the floor.

My vision turned to a tunnel. Was it Blaine? His housekeeper?

As I glanced down at myself, I groaned. I was wearing his freaking clothes, in his freaking bedroom!

The tunnel vision narrowed to a pinpoint. The urge to hide, as ridiculous as that would be, became a fever under my skin. I turned on the spot—a complete circle that achieved nothing besides light respite for my heightened need to do something.

I froze as the footsteps passed the door, a fleeting hope blooming that I might be able to sneak to my own room undetected. How this would help eluded me.

I was still caught in this loop when the footsteps returned, and the door swung open.

Neither of us spoke—I was incapable, and he appeared similarly stunned.

"I was bored with the other windows," I finally said a little vaguely.

His slow perusal went all the way from the tips of my naked toes to my face. His lips tugged up on one side. "Really?"

He thumbed over his shoulder. "I bought you some clothes, but I think I might take them back."

I rationalized that he was teasing me, but I didn't know how to handle his playfulness.

His smile dropped, and the need that burned through in its place brought a thud to my pulse.

"You're a fucking insane level of hot," he said, voice dipping in a way that brought a clench low in my belly.

He was going to fuck me. Whatever he'd intended to do was forgotten. The long duster was yanked off and tossed over a chair before he stalked toward me.

My mind sank into chaos. I turned around like an escape hatch might manifest out of the floor. My heart was pounding, and deep in my core, sore muscles complained.

I was wet. It was like my body knew what was about to happen and was seeking to prepare.

The touch of roughened fingers drawing my hair back over my shoulder brought a stutter to my chest. He was gentle, but I could feel the heat emanating from his body and knew what was to come. "Are you sore, baby?" Head lowering, he pressed a kiss to the exposed flesh at the crux of my shoulder and throat.

"Yes."

"I'll go slowly." Kisses trailed up my throat.

No apology.

No indication that he might let my body recover before he took me again.

His lack of consideration should have appalled me. It didn't. The urgency with which he needed to connect with me lit an equal sense of urgency within me.

His arm looped around my waist from behind. I stared at his big hand, the fingers spread wide over my abdomen were proprietary. His lips nuzzled the side of my throat, sucking against the skin with increasing roughness. I became restless. My sore pussy clenching with every suck-bite. "I like seeing my marks on you," he said between kisses. His hand tightened over my stomach, pinning me to him before his fingers clenched over the material of his T-shirt. "And I fucking love seeing you in my clothes... But I think these need to come off."

His other hand circled me, slipping under the T-shirt and

cupping me over his boxers. It set everything fluttering. Could he feel how wet and ready I was?

He stripped me with slow calculation, spread me out on the bed, and kissed the soreness from my pussy with a reverence that broke me a little. I came under his intimate attention, panting, gasping, and barely cognizant of where I was. As I lay there watching him through lidded eyes, he rose, ripping his T-shirt over his head, toeing off boots, and shucking his pants down.

A brief fumble in the nightstand drawer before he fisted his cock and slathered himself with lube. Then he squirted a generous portion over my pussy, and worked that in as well.

I winced and gasped a little. Tender muscles were forced open as he finger fucked me, stretching and scissoring, working his thumb over my swollen clit until I was a mess of need.

It still hurt when he lined his cock up and sank slowly inside. My muscles locked up at the invasion.

"Relax for me, baby," he said, brushing my hair from my damp face. His hips pumped slowly. My knees lifted to cradle him, allowing him to sink deeper. "That's my good girl. Fuck, you're so hot inside. I'll see if I can get something for the soreness tomorrow."

He began to thrust, slow, determined, but soon building. The pain eased, my body having no choice but to submit.

My mind wasn't far behind. This would not be the only time he would take me tonight. I could feel the urgency in him in the way his lips moved against my throat even as he began to pound into me.

The lack of free will was unexpectedly freeing. My body rose with every thrust, the pleasure overwriting the ache until I spasmed around him in a way that was darkly climactic.

He didn't stop, and my wild moans only drove him to fuck into me harder.

Chapter Fourteen

Nora

I spent the day alone in Carter's apartment, coming to terms with my lot. He'd said he was needed at the medical center and that some things for Adam would be arriving.

They did... oh how they did.

A veritable army turned up at the door, boxes and packages with them. I didn't like to be around men, I fucking hated men, and now I had three huge ones in my home.

My home... this was my home.

My life was so messed up.

It helped that they paid me absolutely no heed as they stomped in and out with the packages, emptied the room Carter had been using as an office and dumped everything in there.

Then I had to sign to say they had done a good job!

Carter called as I was still reeling from this experience and told me not to touch anything until he arrived home.

Carter, who'd been half naked in the bed with me all night.

Carter, whose warm body had been curved around me when I woke.

Carter, who I'd finally admitted somewhere between that fateful meeting at the medical center and now, was the most sinfully attractive man I'd ever met.

Of course, I opened the packages. I couldn't remember being this excited ever as I uncovered all the things a baby might need... new things, nice things, so many things.

I had energy. I couldn't remember the last time I'd had energy, either. The constant stress of Adam's illness and the worry for his next injection had been like a thick, cloying blanket over me for so very long. Life in Sanctuary was also far from a smooth ride. Supplies spilled out into the black market from the communities, and it was always a challenge to source enough food and other things our community needed. The price we paid for our freedom was realized in the uncertainty.

It was disconcerting to find myself in a comfortable home with access to all the food and essentials we might need. A strange and previously unknown determination of hope unfurled inside.

Carter found me on the floor in the middle of his former office. Adam was sitting on a play mat in his new cute romper suit, waving the little teether rattle at Carter before shoving it in his mouth. They had left Carter's computer in the lounge, but everything else had been replaced. The small space was now a perfect child's room with a crib, set of drawers, changing table, and a chest for toys.

"Hey, buddy," Carter said.

Adam immediately offered the slobbery toy to Carter.

"Yeah, I'm going to pass," Carter said, smirking, and I swear that easy moment hit me like a punch in the chest. Then he turned to me, and the smirk dropped. "Your momma and I are going to be having a chat later about her problem following instructions."

I swallowed. Damn that freaking stern doctor voice of his.

"It seemed silly to wait. I—thank you." I was practically gushing. I wanted to roll my eyes at this woman who had invaded my once orderly headspace.

As if I didn't have enough problems, my mind decided to toss out the image of a shirtless Carter from last night.

He left to get changed before my face burned up, and by the time I carried Adam through to the open lounge, I'd dragged some composure back.

It was easy to be around Carter. He was surprisingly patient, even when Adam decided to have a screaming session as I went to put him in the new crib.

Then night came around again and we slept in the same bed. I didn't even pretend to resist when he flung an arm around me and drew my back against his chest.

It felt right. When was the last time someone had held me?

My body and mind hummed with the simple pleasure of feeling safe. I wriggled, subconsciously seeking a closer connection. That was when I felt the hard ridge pressing into my ass.

I froze.

"Ignore it," he said, voice low and a little sleepy, his arm tightening like he sensed I was about to freak out.

I couldn't ignore it. He was a man with ridiculously floppy brown hair, but still a man in possession of that male instrument of destruction.

If I hated men, I hated their cocks more. There was a time when if the opportunity were given, I'd have liberated every living male of that wicked appendage.

Then Adam arrived, and I determined that they were not all bad. Not even his father, Glenn, whom I'd convinced myself I hated, too.

In the darkness of night, as I lay in the embrace of another man, I reflected that I didn't hate Adam's father at all. I loved him, but I hated that he had died and left me alone.

I hated it worse that he'd died trying to protect our unborn child and me.

I'd never cried about it, not once. I cried about Adam, about the lack of ready chocolate, about the sorry state of my thread-bare clothes. But I'd never once acknowledged the depression that had gripped me when that good man left this earthly world.

Maybe all the tears had been about Glenn?

Yeah, I thought that they might have been.

I recalled someone saying once that acknowledging a problem was the first step in its resolution. I hadn't been ready to face my pain before. Memories of the boy who became a man and who stuck with me throughout the dark years after the collapse were too painful. Today, as Carter's warm oh-so-strong body curved around mine, I thought about Glenn a lot.

Despite my painful emotional awakening, I managed to get some sleep.

All too soon, it was time for me to start my job. Strong, undeterminable emotions gripped me when Carter drew out the brander that hung on a chain around his neck and turned to Adam with intent. "He needs an owner," he said. "Until he comes of age and can take one of his own."

Adam had never had an owner. Never had a male figure to look out for him.

My nod was swift, fluttery nerves low in my belly. I didn't want my baby's perfect skin to bear any mark. And yet, it wasn't a terrible mark. I'd even looked at mine for the first time yesterday, bracing myself for the aversion that never came.

The deed was done swiftly. Adam barely fussed.

"He's mine now," Carter said, eyes lifting from Adam to me. "Both of you are mine."

Chapter Fifteen

Blaine

I hadn't seen Carter since he'd put my brand on Ava, but word had reached me that he'd claimed ownership of another woman from Sanctuary.

Carter, who had zero interest in ownership.

Carter, who had zero interest in babies in any form or proximity, had taken on both a mother and a child.

I'd no interest in them either before Ava blundered into my life. She wasn't on any birth control, according to Carter's report. As soon as I'd read that little side note, I'd been obsessed with planting my seed in her belly, and I was fucking into her sore pussy every chance I got.

There were rules around challenges. During pregnancy and for a year after, you couldn't be challenged. It suited Taylor's plans to have an expanding population. While the lack of challenge to my ownership was an appealing benefit, I just wanted her good and knocked up.

She had yet to leave my home. I knew that I'd have to let

her out eventually or she would go crazy in the apartment alone. But every time I walked in the door, I had her under me and was fucking her into next week.

We barely spoke. Not the best way to create a lasting relationship, which was clearly what I wanted given I was determined to put my kid in her belly. But I couldn't think straight when I was around her.

I'd have appreciated some respite from Taylor's domination plans, but his most recent and largest acquisition was far from accepting of its fate. Trouble had kicked off. A small pocket of resistance had holed up in the southern slums, and it had taken the better part of three days to clear it out.

Every inch of my body was battered and bruised. I was soaked through—all it did was fucking rain at this time of year. It had been three days since I'd been home, slept in my own bed, and enjoyed the luxury of feeling clean. At least I'd had the foresight to give Ava a cell phone and had spoken to her twice. Now that order was restored, all I wanted to do was take a shower, eat, sleep, and make sure my woman hadn't caused any trouble in no particular order.

The message to report to Taylor immediately could not have come at a worse time. If fresh troubles had started, I was going to unleash hell.

I found Taylor in his office, relaxed in his leather wingback chair behind an equally pretentious desk. A tumbler of whiskey rested on the leather top. To his left, rain-splattered windows distorted the nighttime city lights.

He wasn't alone. Sitting opposite was the political worm, Frank Hurst.

Hurst's lips curled in a sneer as he inspected me. I was still wearing my fatigues and body armor, which were filthy, torn up in places and spattered with mud and blood.

"Been fraternizing with the locals again, Blaine?" Hurst

said. "I think you actually enjoy playing thug. Lucky for you that Taylor's conquests provide you with the opportunity. You always were more cage fighter material."

"Fuck off, Hurst," I replied. I was head and shoulders above him when he was standing and had at least a hundred pounds over him. Given how many verbal altercations we'd had over the years, I had no problem with blatant intimidation.

Taylor chuckled. The self-appointed king might be intelligent, but he was also a psycho and loved nothing better than a little sparring between his close ranks.

"You better leave us to talk, Frank." Taylor's grin was all teeth. "He's looking pissed, and I suspect my news is going to piss him off even more. You probably don't want to be here when that happens." He may be talking to Hurst, but it was me he stared at with calculation in his eyes.

What the fuck was he about to tell me?

Was it something to do with Ava?

I kept my expression carefully neutral, but inside, adrenaline was flooding my system in preparation for a battle. The question of who Ava was before I'd stumbled across her rose once more. I'd known I was getting into a bullshit situation when I saw the lack of mark.

I'd gone there anyway. If anyone tried to separate us, the fallout would not be pretty. My palms turned clammy—enhancements could be counterproductive. The need to return home and check that she was safe and well felt like ants crawling under my skin.

The chair creaked under Hurst. He seemed caught up in his desire to watch me get my bad news. But he was also a man with a healthy sense of self-preservation, which had kept him as Taylor's right-hand man where so many others had failed.

Rising gracefully, he placed an empty glass on the table.

"No problem. I still think you should consider getting a muzzle for your dog when you bring him inside."

I huffed out a laugh. "Better hope Taylor never cuts one of us loose, Hurst, because thirty seconds later, you're dead." I enjoyed watching him take a wide step around me as he exited the room.

As the door clicked shut, I returned my attention to Taylor. His contemplative expression said the news would be bad enough for me to forget all about breaking Hurst's jaw.

"I had an interesting visitor," he said. "A woman who has recently joined us from Sanctuary has issued a challenge for Ava."

I felt my brows pinch together. "What the fuck? A woman? Her sister, maybe?"

"Indeed, a woman, and no, not a blood relative. She looked —" he paused to shrug, "—like she could handle herself. Mitch said she's enhanced. He's recommended her for the forces once she passes the probation period."

My eyebrows crawled into my hairline. "You're shitting me? She wants to challenge me?" The adrenaline was still ripping through my system, and the lack of action was making me a little woozy. Maybe if I'd taken the time to talk to Ava instead of fucking her, I'd know what this was about. "Does she even know who I am or anything about me?"

Taylor smiled. "I did try to dissuade her, but she shrugged as if to say 'who cares', and on reflection, it would be such an interesting encounter. Besides, didn't I hear that you were looking to offload her?"

He said this so matter-of-fact that I had to fight the urge to punch the son-of-a-bitch.

"I may do," I said. I'd played down my first foray into ownership, having learned a long time ago to keep my cards close to my chest with Taylor. If he suspected my level of obsession with Ava, he'd find a way to use it to his advantage. "When I'm ready. Are you going to let the challenge stand?"

"I am," Taylor replied. "I'm sure it's nothing you can't handle. I've no grounds to refuse... unless Ava can persuade her 'friend' to retract. Sure, it's a little unusual for a woman to be an owner, but what makes an owner? You just need to make a claim and hold it."

An epiphany hit me that was both unwelcome and disconcerting. "You think they're in a relationship?" I asked, already half convinced of the answer. A friend would ask to see Ava, not challenge the appointed head of Taylor's forces. Something had been off right from the start with Ava. She said she hadn't been with someone for years, and I'd wondered how the fuck that was possible. She couldn't look after herself, not even close, so someone else was.

"You mean, did they fuck?" Taylor's blunt statement hit a raw nerve. "I would say so. The woman who marched in here had the look of more than a concerned friend. *Rabid* is the word that comes to mind."

Well, fuck that.

A possessive rage I didn't know I harbored rose up and demanded my attention.

After that first time when I'd fucked Ava, she'd sobbed like her heart was breaking. I scrubbed a hand in my hair. "When?"

"It should be now," Taylor replied. "But I'll give you a few hours."

My grunt was derisive. I'd gone three straight days with no more than snatches of sleep. I felt sick with fatigue, and my body was teetering on the point of shutting down. Three hours wasn't enough, not for a credible challenge.

I could see it in Taylor's face, this was going to be a credible challenge.

"I need to talk to Ava," I said.

He inclined his head, magnanimous... anticipating the showdown. "The cage, o-six-hundred hours. Unless you can dissuade her."

The cage was public—the place where the higher ranks dealt with challenges. I'd been in the cage before, but never over a woman.

Did I really want to challenge someone that Ava cared about?

Was I even capable of meeting that challenge in my current physical state?

Could I let her go?

A primal instinct gripped me at the thought of losing her.

One thing was sure, I wasn't giving her up without a fight. I just didn't know what kind of fight that might be.

Chapter Sixteen

Ava

He'd been gone for three days, and I was ready to climb the walls.

If not for the sweet housekeeper who had come around to clean up and stock the fridge, I might have done something stupid... like try to leave the apartment.

At least I had some clothes now, so that was something. The leggings and tops were functional, but they were also clean and fit me.

I don't know who'd been more surprised when the sweet young woman entered, her or me. It didn't help matters that her heavy Eastern European accent and broken English made communication a challenge. She could understand me better than she could speak, but I got enough of it to realize that she was here to clean his home.

Which was ridiculous given I was literally here all the time and had absolutely nothing to do but stare out the window.

Owned

I'd hacked into his computer yesterday after his second call to check on me, which had yielded nothing.

He didn't say much during the call. Asked me how I was. Promised to take me out once he was back.

That was a lie.

We both knew the minute he entered the door, I'd be underneath him, all too willing and eager for the only thing that felt right in this crazy world.

Then yesterday, I'd started my period, and I knew I was in trouble when the first feeling was one of disappointment, not relief.

Oh, how I'd fallen. I swear Blaine only needed to look at me, and my pussy drooled in anticipation.

So it came as quite a surprise when he returned, and sex wasn't the first thing on his mind.

The man who entered the apartment was the same man I'd met on the rooftop. It was like I'd forgotten what he was over the last few weeks... had it only been a few weeks? This time, he hadn't gotten changed or cleaned up. This time he was in full combat kit, weapons and all. The coppery tang of blood, smoke, and gasoline surrounded him. The man was a walking advertisement for death, and his face was stone cold.

A prickling awareness skittered under my skin. My smile dropped. I stood on one side of the couch and Blaine on the other. Normally, he'd have tossed his duster over the couch and would be offloading weapons into his storage drawer by now.

Something was wrong, very wrong. I didn't know what yet.

"Who exactly is Jodi, and why is she issuing me with a challenge?" Blaine demanded, voice every bit as cold as his demeanor.

Relief, panic, and hope beat at me in a confused jumble. "She's here? In Guilder?" My face went cold then hot. *Challenge?*

"You didn't answer my question," he said.

The gap between us was no more than ten paces, but it might as well have been a bottomless chasm.

Jodi was here, safe, well... and issuing a challenge to Blaine. I swallowed. "She's a friend. She took care of me."

"A friend? What sort of a friend? Do you love her?"

My chest rose on an unsteady breath. The man was a seething tower of deadly intent. This could not happen. He could not be about to fight Jodi for ownership of me. I was no fool; he would destroy her.

Inside, little pieces were crumbling. *Oh, Jodi, why would you do this... and with Blaine?* I'd known she would do something stupid, but this exceeded all my expectations.

His eyes never left mine. His rage was palpable, and I wondered what the hell Jodi had said.

"I do." His fists clenched at his side, and his jaw locked so tight, it was a wonder it didn't crack. The door was open; no choice but to walk through. "But not in the way I used to. I suppose I was in awe of her for a long time, and felt such gratitude that for many years, I confused it with something more."

My mouth was dust dry. I'd been alone for three days— plenty of time to think things through. Then yesterday when I'd realized I wasn't pregnant, it threw me for a loop. Jodi had always been there, an undemanding protector. I owed her everything. I felt guilty as hell for even sleeping with Blaine.

Facts and feelings could not be ignored, though, no matter how painful they were. Somewhere along the line, Jodi had become a friend, a very dear friend I'd shared intimacy with, but still a friend and no more.

A tic thumped in his jaw, and he didn't speak for the longest time.

"I don't want you to fight her." A tear trickled down my

cheek, soon followed by another. "Please, don't fight her," I whispered.

"I don't have a fucking choice," he said. "I can't fucking let you go." He tossed the helmet he'd been holding onto a nearby chair. "Do you want to be with her?"

I started to speak then stopped. I'd no idea what to say or how to better articulate myself without prostrating myself at his feet. Sickness churned in my gut. I missed Jodi. Had Blaine asked me this question weeks ago when I'd first arrived, I'd have jumped at the chance to be with her, and would be begging him for precisely that.

In the short time since I'd met him, he'd been relentless and uncompromising—he wanted me, so he took me—no apology and no discussion. But he'd also been patient within those bounds. Had never once hurt me, even after I'd punched him on that desolate rooftop.

Many men would have hurt me at such a time, slapped, or even beaten me to teach me my place. But this wasn't even gratitude that he wasn't a monster, it was so much more complex.

I tried to unpick my feelings to test if this was some warped primal programming to upgrade Jodi as a protector.

I couldn't say exactly what I felt for Blaine. There wasn't enough time for it to be love, but it was still a potent emotion.

Obsession? Possibly.

Lust? Definitely. But there was more to it than that.

Blaine

She still hadn't answered me and I couldn't quantify precisely why a dead space seemed to be opening up somewhere inside me. I was just pissed that someone else had laid claim to her affection. The selfish bastard that I was, I wanted it all. She wasn't entirely immune to me. She responded to me—she had fucking come all over my cock.

But she still hadn't answered my question.

And I still didn't know what the fuck I was going to do.

A clock was ticking. I needed to address the challenge; there was no getting out of that.

Maybe she had been playing me, trying not to piss me off while waiting for her girlfriend to come to the rescue.

My gut clenched. I couldn't shake off a sick feeling that I'd been taken for a fool.

Her breath hitched—perhaps my face was revealing how unhinged I was, but before I could demand an answer, she rounded the couch and walked all the way up to me.

There was a brief hesitation when she reached me before she caught my face between her trembling hands and drawing my face down, pressed her lips against mine.

The shock immobilized me. Not once had she been the instigator—I hadn't given her the chance. I'd thought of little else but her for the last three days. It felt like forever since I'd been inside her. I wanted her to want me with the same feral passion I felt toward her.

Then my brain finally kicked in against the drug of her soft lips, and fisting a handful of her hair, I pulled her away.

She was breathing heavily. We both were.

"You better not be doing this to stop me kicking your girl-friend's ass." My voice sounded like gravel. I was so close to losing it. My basal side didn't give a fuck about her reasons, but I was damned if I was going to be used, however satisfying the process may be.

"You think I don't want this? Don't want you?" She shook her head, hands shaking against my face. If she was acting, then it was worthy of a pre-war Oscar.

"I guess I was afraid at first," she paused. "It had been such a long time since I was with a man... You're not exactly like the men I once knew." Her hands slipped down. I didn't like the distancing one fucking bit. "I still wanted you, even at first... And you never asked me about the before."

"I'm asking now. And you still haven't answered the fucking question."

She flinched, lashes lowering, but I refused to let her go. The feel of her against me, the clean scent, the silken hair under my rough fingers were like a hook tearing into the last remnants of my self-control.

"We've known each other a few weeks," she said, eyes flashing to meet mine with accusation. "And you've been away for three fucking days."

"Do you want to be with her or me?"

"You!"

The sound I made was something like a growl. I swear that was the longest ten minutes of my life while she skirted around a response. I tightened my fist in her hair and planted my mouth over hers before she could say another word. The clock was ticking, but I felt fucking invincible in the wake of her admission, and all I could think about was getting inside her.

Hoisting her up into my arms, I stalked toward the couch. Dropping her on her back and fighting to free enough of my kit so I could get my aching cock out.

"Blaine, wait—"

I'd ripped her leggings and panties off before she finished talking, which was when I saw the blood.

I stopped dead.

"I didn't have anything..."

She trailed off as I stared at the bloody smears knowing what it meant. "This won't be happening again for a good long while." Lining my cock up, I thrust deep inside.

Her little whimper said I'd been too rough. "I know, baby." I smoothed the hair back from her face, kissing her long and deep to try and distract her. Her pussy felt like a hot vise pulsing around my cock. I hadn't moved yet and I was close to shooting my load. "You've tightened up. Try and relax for me." A few pounding thrusts later and she was clawing at my ass and lifting her hips to meet every thrust.

It was fast, hot, dirty, and I didn't give a damn. My thumb found her clit as I sucked bites against her throat. "Come for me, Ava. Come now. Come all over my cock."

A few more deep, soul-crushing thrusts, and she did, mouth open on a moan I felt all the way to my balls. The feeling of those tight muscles milking my cock tipped me right over with her. I couldn't stop fucking coming.

I peppered kisses up her throat and across her cheeks before taking her lips.

It was hard to leave her warmth—the couch was going to be a hell of a mess, but I would worry about that later.

Hauling myself off her, I took a seat and dragged her limp body onto my lap.

I checked my watch—one fucking hour. Taking out my cell, I handed it to her. "Her number's at the top. Call her and tell her to back off."

She went to hop down.

"Not fucking happening," I growled, putting her right back on my lap, and catching her chin so that she was forced to meet my eyes. "If you can't convince her, I'll have no choice but to fight. This community is civilized for the most part. But a challenge is a challenge, and you accept it, or you forfeit. I have one hour before the challenge, so whatever you need to say to her, you need to make it fast and compelling."

"Okay," she said. "I'll convince her."

There was hesitation in her voice, though, like she wasn't

sure about the outcome. The crazy ex-girlfriend had been bold enough to gain an audience with Taylor, and I figured she wouldn't be easy to convince.

Whatever Ava's relationship with Jodi, or those men she had known long ago, I intended to erase all of it from her memory.

***

Ava

I burst out crying when I heard Jodi's voice.

It took several deep breaths before I could get anything out, and even then, it was barely coherent. I wasn't lying to Blaine when I'd said I wanted to be with him, but damn it, this was hard.

I told Jodi I was okay, that I was just happy to hear her voice. As was typical for Jodi, she went off on a wild rant about what she was going to do and who she was going to kill.

"Jodi, please! I need you to hear me out. Can you do that?"

Her sigh was loud. I could picture her grinding her teeth, jaw locked and eyes spitting fire. It didn't help that I was on Blaine's lap, covered in filth, blood, and cum, and naked from the waist down. His cock nestled under my ass was like an attention magnet.

"I don't want you to fight Blaine."

Jodi huffed out another breath, probably rolling her damn eyes.

"He's not a bad man." God help me, could this get any more embarrassing. I had a bad feeling he could hear both sides of the conversation. I risked a glance; his locked jaw said he could. I lowered my lashes. "He's—I think he's a good one." *Maybe the best I've met since I left that nightmare with my uncle.* "Please, Jodi. Can you give it time?" *I think I love him. I know one day soon I'll need to leave, but I want to pretend for a little while.*

"Is he there with you now?" she demanded. "Because that's fucking coercion if he is, and I'm going to kick the bastard's ass from here to next week."

"If you fight, Jodi, it's going to destroy me." Blaine's fingers tightened painfully on my waist. He was getting ready to rip the cell from me; I knew it. "Don't do this, Jodi. Don't fucking destroy me." My anger imploded, and I said the one thing I knew would get through. "I'll never forgive you if you do."

"Fucking Christ!" she hissed through the cell. "Fine. Fucking fine. Just promise me you're okay. Say the words. Say you fucking promise. And don't lie to me or so help me, I'll kick your ass too."

"I'm fine, Jodi, I promise. Please, withdraw the challenge."

"You're not giving me a choice, are you? I'll do it. But I need to see you soon."

The phone was wrested from my fingers. "You'll see Ava when I damn well say," Blaine barked into the phone. "And if you go off upsetting her again, that may be the wrong side of never. Are we clear?"

I could hear Jodi roaring down the cell. He winced and mouthed the words *crazy bitch,* before surprising me by smirking.

There'd been many surreal moments since I'd met Blaine, but I thought this one might have topped the chart.

"Yes, I'll be there tomorrow. Looking forward to meeting you too."

He snapped the cell off and tossed it to the couch beside us. "I'm so fucking exhausted."

Yes, so was I. "Let's go to bed."

Chapter Seventeen

Nora

Apparently, something in the tests I'd undertaken suggested I was a good fit for a job at the medical center.

In Sanctuary, everyone had a job to do, a myriad of activities that kept the place functioning, clean, and the community members fed. But this felt different. A job that came with a wage, of sorts. I'd not heard of anyone having a paid job, not since before the collapse, and that was such a long time ago.

There was a day care facility at the medical center, and I was never more than ten minutes away from Adam the whole time, but I cried my heart out the first day, and it wasn't much better the next.

By the end of the first week, it wasn't quite as terrifying, although I still checked on him seventeen times.

While in Sanctuary, I'd left Adam with Rachel on plenty of occasions. The medical center was different. I didn't know anyone here, except for Carter. And there were so many people, it terrified me how many. But the day care was surprisingly well presented, catering for older babies through to school age.

I was shocked to discover they had schools in Guilder City, and further, attendance was mandatory.

It was a lot to take in. The opportunities presented to Adam living here far surpassed those within Sanctuary. And unexpectedly, and although I had only known Carter for a short time, I thought he might make a good role model.

My hospital duties involved stocking the essential medical supplies for the wards. The first morning, another assistant shadowed me to show me how it was done and how everything was recorded.

After that, I was left to do the work unsupervised, mostly. It became apparent early on that new arrivals were watched. I was okay with that. Time would bring my acceptance, and I ignored the few people who acted coldly toward me.

I visited each medical bay, checked the supplies, and restocked where necessary. It wasn't a complicated task, but everything had to be documented and updated into the stock system. It was satisfying.

Lunch and breaks were spent with Adam, where I met a few mothers whose shifts coincided with mine. They were more welcoming than the ward staff, and I soon found myself looking forward to seeing the other moms as much as I enjoyed doing my work. I was at the bottom of the food chain here, not a nurse or doctor, but I did my part to make sure everything ran smoothly.

It was far from an easy ride, but it wasn't terrible either.

But my new life was thrust once more into the dark space by the arrival of Mandy's sister, Gilly. The same mean, pinched expression as her sister, she cornered me in the supply room, shutting the door and putting her back against it.

I knew Carter had slept with her; he'd been brutally blunt about this while explaining Mandy's behavior.

"I heard Carter's looking to hand you off to someone more appropriate for an outsider girl like you," Gilly said. "My advice—don't get comfortable. He doesn't want you or your brat."

Her words hurt; I couldn't lie to myself, but my arms still folded, and my infamous temper reared its head. I'd been scared of many things since the world collapsed. Gilly wasn't one of them. "I figured you couldn't be as big of a bitch as your sister. Guess I was wrong."

She laughed. "That the best you've got? I have a lot of friends here. They'll be sure to watch that you don't try to steal anything. Outsiders can't help themselves. The laws are strict. Those who can't fit in find themselves back outside the gates where they belong. I told Carter he shouldn't be so charitable." She smirked. "I'd have said more, but he has a way of distracting me, you know?"

No, I really didn't know, and I didn't want to either. Maybe he was still intimate with her? It wasn't like he was acting on his ownership rights with me.

I convinced myself I didn't want him to and that I wasn't ready. But the truth was that I was jealous. I wanted to say more, but I curbed it because I didn't know the way of things here yet. I was still finding my feet, and I hated that she might be able to spoil that. Gilly left, ass sashaying as she gloated over her prowess in knocking me down.

Pulling myself together, I got on with my afternoon rounds. One rotten apple didn't make a disaster.

But two did.

The man occupying the bed of 17E had a knife wound. As I blundered into the cubical, I knew I'd made a mistake.

"That real red hair?" he asked.

I thought about lying. I wasn't one for being tongue-tied, but there was something about the way he was sizing me up that set the hair on the back of my neck rising.

"I'll take that as a yes," he said.

He was similar in age to me, stocky build, with a drawn face that I'd come to associate with drugs. In that instant, I was thrown back into that time after Glenn and before Sanctuary when I'd found myself the unwitting guest of a gang.

The nurse's uniform didn't do much to disguise the size of my breasts, and the man's lecherous gaze went straight there.

I shuddered, frozen with my fear of those ghosts from my past.

"You got an owner, sweet cheeks?"

"Yes," I said, lowering my head and nearly dropping the supplies in my haste to check the supply caddy at his bedside.

His hand closing over mine was shocking. I didn't like to be touched, but especially not by men... any man other than Carter.

"I look after my girls," he said, confirming my worst suspicions.

I snatched my hand from his.

"I have an owner." It surprised me how much comfort I took from this statement when the idea had appalled me not so long ago.

He smirked, not bothered.

"Let me know his name. I'll talk to him. My customers would pay well for a natural redhead with a bit of fire." He winked. "Not to mention that fucking rack."

"Go to hell, you sick fuck." I shoved the drawer shut so violently the caddy shook. "I have a baby. Men like you don't want that complication."

His eyes immediately dropped to my chest again. "Nah." He grinned. "You'd be surprised what clients pay for. You still breastfeeding? They pay extra for that. How about you let me know your owner's name, and we can have a little chat?"

He cracked his knuckles.

Why was this cretin even receiving medical attention?

"Doctor Carter is her owner."

I glanced back over my shoulder, already knowing who that haughty voice belonged to. Gilly, whom Carter had been inside, was every bit as bitchy as her sister in allocations. God help me, I wanted to hurl at the mere thought of Carter and Gilly together. What did he see in the tasteless hussy?

I mentally scoffed at myself. Her perfect blue eyes and her perfect auburn hair neatly tied back were plenty enough. I doubt there were stretch marks on the perfect figure she was rocking in her nurse's uniform.

"Doctor?" The man on the bed said, disdain dripping from his tone. "You're shitting me. Not even military? How's he hope to hold on to a pretty little thing like you?"

The blood drained from my face.

Gilly was inspecting me like she had a dirty smell under her nose. "He felt sorry for her," she said. "So I heard. I'm sure he'd be only too happy to hand her off."

Hands shaking around the supply cart, I backed out of the cubical. Somehow, I got through my rounds, although I was quaking the whole time.

I had forced Carter into this. I could see a mile off that he was a good man. He hadn't once tried to force me and had been patient with Adam even when he'd screamed the place down. So yeah, it was within the bounds of possibility that he was doing what he thought was right in offering me ownership.

Why would he want to keep me?

I told myself that a good man like Carter would not hand me over to a pimp.

Then I remembered that he was a doctor, not even a

soldier, and I wondered what he could possibly do if the thug in cubical 17E decided to pursue ownership.

I worried all day, grateful when it was time to collect Adam and return home.

I should tell Carter what had happened. But I was so relieved by his smile and the way he stopped to give attention to Adam that I couldn't bring myself to sully it.

Soon, we would be home and safe, and I could forget all about 17E and his words.

Carter

I knew something was off as soon as I met Nora at the end of her shift. I figured it was something to do with Gilly, who'd found reasons to speak to me over recent days that defied logic.

Today, I'd had enough and told her to get on with her fucking job.

I'd created a monster with that woman. She might be hot, convenient, and have an owner who had no issues offering her up. Half the hospital had dipped in that hole. I knew she saw me as a potential owner upgrade. I wasn't delusional enough to think I was the only doctor she was pursuing, nor to presume her social climb would stop at me. Gilly was playing a dangerous game, but that was her problem, not mine.

It had been fun, but things had changed after a broken, sassy redhead entered my life.

I questioned my decision to become Nora's owner as often as I questioned how long I could keep my hands off her. I'd been waking up with a stone hard dick every morning since she had first gotten into my bed—I didn't have faith in my ability to hold out much longer.

Owned

The kid screaming certainly helped keep my libido under control, as did his mother, who fluctuated between abrasive and sweet without much in the way of warning.

Okay, the kid was cute sometimes. Except for three am this morning when he decided to projectile vomit all over the crib. I still couldn't get the smell out of my nose.

I found Nora cute all the time, even when she was glaring daggers at me. But especially the softer side of her... the side I imagined I'd see more of once I'd pounded her pussy.

Ownership. According to Blaine, it might be wrong, and while I usually respected his opinion as the source of greater knowledge than mine, I saw it in a whole new and twisted light.

Also, he'd lost that shiny accolade when he'd gone over to the dark side and claimed ownership over Ava.

My new status as owner consumed every moment of downtime. I wanted in Nora's hot little pussy. I wanted in that tight little ass that my cock nestled against every night, and I wanted in that sassy mouth with the pink pouty lips more than I wanted my next breath.

For reasons I could not explain, knowing that I was her owner, that I could have her in any way I wanted to, made everything hotter than hell.

I considered myself a measured man. Anarchy was always waiting on the periphery. The rules of society dictated that we temper our animalistic side lest we all fall back into that uncivilized void. Retaining that vital connection to reason was getting harder every time I was near her. She was attracted to me. I'd seen hints along the way. She certainly didn't hesitate to sprawl all over me in the bed. Maybe she was wondering what was taking me so long?

I could barely think straight during the day. Maybe after I'd been inside her, I'd be able to think straight again.

It was with this burgeoning tension that we exited the medical center into the underground garage.

A welcoming committee was waiting—the kind that set my teeth on edge and adrenaline surging through my blood.

Blaine wasn't the only one who'd had enhancements. Within the bounds of my work, I'd taken everything I could. But I was no soldier and wasn't expecting to have to defend my ownership rights this soon. It didn't help that I'd spent half the night restless with a hard-on and the other cleaning up vomit.

I eyed the two beat-up ex-military SUV's, the dozen lowlifes, and the nervous guy with a datapad and glasses who awaited me. James, the asshole, wasn't among them, but then again, James had seemed like a decent kind of guy, and it was becoming clear that these were not.

"Babe, have you been speaking to anyone who might issue a challenge since this morning?"

She was white as a sheet and clutching Adam to her chest, arms around him like a shield. Her mouth opened and closed, and no words came out.

I'm so screwed.

Placing my hand on her shoulder, I put my body between her and the threat. "It's going to be alright," I said. But in truth, I didn't know if it would ever be alright again. The garage was eerily quiet for this time of day. I'd heard rumors that this was happening—men pursuing ownership the uncivilized way. Not that there was anything civilized about a regular challenge, but these 'unofficial' ones that took place in the presence of a bought adjudicator were particularly heinous.

"He was being treated for a stab wound," Nora said, voice a whisper. She swallowed. "I didn't tell him. A nurse did."

Nurse? Yes, I could guess who that would be, and that bitch would be seeing a side of me she didn't like.

But first, I had to get through this.

I could feel Nora's shoulder trembling under my fingers, or was that me?

How long had it been since I'd done more than spar with Blaine? I'd been eleven, still a kid when we arrived here, and that was the last time I'd fought for my life.

Only I wasn't fighting for my life tonight; I was fighting for Nora and Adam. How did they even set this up? Taking my cell from my pocket, I jabbed a message to Blaine. The chances of him being anywhere near were slight, but I'd grasp at anything under the circumstance.

No answer came.

The dick with the datapad called out my name and issued the formal request.

I shoved my cell in Nora's hands. "Keep an eye on it. I've messaged my brother. Answer him for me while I—" *Get the shit kicked out of me.* "—deal with this." With a final squeeze to Nora's shoulder, I turned around.

I could take one asshole. I was pissed enough that I thought I could probably take two. But I couldn't take ten.

I huffed out a breath as I took it all in. "A challenge? Are you for fucking real? I've owned her for all of a few weeks."

The man who stepped forward looked like a junkie with his nervous, twitchy energy. The rest didn't look much better.

"The challenge is issued," the deadbeat said, giving me an up-down look that said my chances of winning were slim. "The pretty little nurse said you were tougher than you looked." He thumbed in the direction of his back up. "Bitch sold me a lie." He shrugged. "Feel free to walk away. No one will know but us that you didn't take a punch."

I kept my eyes on him as I slipped my jacket off.

A few weeks. I'd been an owner for a few weeks, and I was already about to fuck up. James probably had a dozen buddies he could call on if shit like this happened. What did I have? A few studious doctors... and Blaine... and Blaine was always busy. I hadn't messaged or spoken to him since he collected Ava from the medical facility.

He was going to kick my ass worse than these low-lifes were about to when he found out what had happened.

The whirr of the ventilation fans was broken by the growl of an incoming vehicle. All heads turned that direction. Whoever had stumbled into this situation would get the hell out once they realized what was going down.

The Humvee that came into view was familiar. I grinned as it pulled up... and Blaine jumped out. Full combat gear and the ever-present arsenal of weapons. He was muddy and bloody— I'd never seen a more welcome sight.

I heard Nora gasp behind me, but I didn't have time for an explanation.

Blaine's sweeping gaze took in the whole situation.

"Fuck off," my opponent said. "Nothing for you here."

Blaine chuckled—that was my asshole brother that I loved, right there. "A couple of your buddies made the mistake of trying to dissuade me from entering. I killed them," he said.

Not a hint of emotion played on his face. Slamming the Humvee door shut, he leaned back against it and folded his arms.

Relief washed over me. If they tried anything, he would have my back. That was all I needed.

He smirked and mouthed, *fuck the asshole up.*

It would be my pleasure.

My fingers no longer shook as I undid my shirt and peeled it off. The T-shirt underneath was close-fitting and easier to move in.

"Eh, you're packing a lot of fire-power," the nervous adjudicator said. "This is a clean challenge between two parties. We don't want any trouble here."

Blaine snorted out a huff. "Clean?"

I was confident the adjudicator's days were numbered. Soon, he'd be lugging rocks in the infamous pit or starting a new life outside. "He's good to take down one asshole," Blaine said. "I'm here as an unofficial observer, to make sure nothing underhand goes on. Taylor has been taking a special interest in these 'clean' challenges. He's been busy with his recent acquisition. Looks like his home turf has been suffering from neglect. I'll be sure to update him when we talk this evening."

"Bullshit!" the thug said. Only, I was sure he didn't believe it was bullshit. Blaine had a way of projecting deadly intent. His relaxed stance invaded me—I could do this.

Turning, I passed my shirt and jacket to a shaken Nora. "It's my brother, Blaine," I said quietly with a wink. "I promise it'll be okay." This time the words felt like the truth. "Go and stand with him while I do this. He won't let anything happen to you. No matter what happens."

Go hard and go early, Blaine had always said when referring to a challenge. He wasn't talking about an ownership challenge at the time, but I could see that it applied. *Leave them with a strong message as to why they shouldn't fuck with you or yours ever again.*

I was going to go so fucking hard, the asshole daring to issue a corrupt challenge would have to be carried out of here.

"Your brother?" Nora asked, eyeing Blaine like he was the grim reaper... which wasn't that far from the truth.

"Yeah, my brother," I said, and there was pride in my voice.

Nora

A group of men were waiting for us in the dark underground garage. One of them, all too familiar.

I had handled the situation with the man in the medical center poorly. I should have left the moment he showed interest in me, returned to the storeroom, and waited there. Or called Carter. He'd told me to call him if anything troubled me. If only I'd spoken to him before we left, we might not have walked into this trap. And I knew it was a set-up, no explanation required.

Then the Humvee had rumbled into the garage, and I was sure things couldn't get any worse.

That terrifying man was Carter's brother, and the balance had been tipped back. I searched for similarities between the floppy-haired doctor and the hardened, much older soldier leaning casually against the Humvee radiating menace.

I thought there was none, but as Carter turned away from me and approached his opponent and the first blow fell, I realized I didn't know the unassuming doctor at all.

The fight was fast and vicious. The meaty thud of fists connecting with flesh, the hoarse grunts, and all too soon, the splatter of blood ejected from torn flesh. I didn't see Blaine move, but then he was beside me, and I took comfort from his shadow. I swallowed, sickened, and yet unable to look away, unwilling to look away. This was Carter, a side of him I might never have known if not for this challenge.

He was winning; I could see this. The thug's buddies could see it too. Their restless stance, the way they cast nervous glances our way as if assessing Blaine's potential threat. They called out to their man, crude encouragements, jeers, and demands to 'end the pussy doctor'.

Their man was losing.

Had Carter's brother not arrived, they would have acted. I was shaking so violently; the closeness of this terrible fate and the precarious nature of what would unfold was acid in my gut.

"Interfere, and I will end every one of you," Blaine said.

He meant it. I didn't know how he would enact this threat, but the pimp's buddies sensed his conviction.

They grew agitated.

"Don't fucking quit, Carter," Blaine growled. "That asshole dared to dirty challenge. I want to see his blood all over the fucking floor."

I sobbed quietly, clutching Adam to my chest as the pimp went down. Carter went with him, raining blow after blow.

Finally, I looked away from the bloody pulp. The men jeered louder, promising to come back and cut Carter in his sleep.

"Try it, assholes," Blaine said. I opened my eyes to see him wade into the carnage and drag Carter off the prone man.

Carter fought wildly, but Blaine had him in a neck lock, and the fight went out of him. "Clear your shit up and get the fuck out of Guilder City," Blaine said. "If I find any of you inside Taylor's jurisdiction twenty-four hours from now, I won't hesitate to shoot."

They hefted the broken man up off the floor and fled the scene like the rats they were.

The warbling whirr of the extractor fans and the harsh saw of Carter's breathing were the only sounds left. Blaine slowly released his younger brother but kept a steadying hand on his shoulder as Carter turned toward me.

It took every drop of will power not to flinch away when the sight broke my heart. His poor face battered and swollen, the raw knuckles... and the blood.

Heaving in a breath, Carter nodded to Blaine. "I'm good."

"You're damn right you're fucking good," Blaine said. "Like

a fucking animal." Blaine smirked as Carter swiped the blood trickling from his nose. "You're going to feel like a trainwreck tomorrow."

"I don't think it'll take that long," Carter said. His soft voice was so familiar and at odds with this fierce battle-scarred warrior who stood before me.

I wanted the closeness of connection, yet was terrified of hurting him, and unsure of myself when the only place we touched was within the darkened bedroom at the end of the day.

"Come here," Carter said, and I lost the hesitation, throwing my arms around his neck. Adam made his little baby noises of complaint when he was jostled between us.

"Leave the car," Blaine said. "I'll take you home and have someone collect it for you. Unless you need to head back into the medical center."

"I don't need medical treatment. I just want to go home," Carter said. His hands were still tight against my waist as he eased back slightly.

I knew in that instant that everything had changed.

Chapter Eighteen

Blaine

As I drove the Humvee out of the medical center garage and into the damp, dark streets that perpetuated Guilder City at this time of year, I reflected that things could have gone so much worse.

That I'd only just got to the medical center in time was not lost on me. The thought of Carter dealing with that scum alone made me want to go on a fucking rampage. Thankfully, someone had tipped me off when the security footage was cut. I'd been heading that way on a hunch when his message had arrived.

I cut a glance to my left, catching his grin. I fucking loved the idiot, and I was so proud of the way he'd handled himself, not shirking at what needed to be done.

Sure, I could have waded in. It would have been easy to shoot the lot of them, the corrupt adjudicator included. But if Carter was going to assume the role of an owner to a pretty redhead, he was going to need to fight. Better to go hard and send a message to the next asshole who thought he could challenge.

Carter had done exactly that.

"How old's the baby?" I asked.

"Jesus, Blaine," he muttered, throwing a look over his shoulder to the back where Nora and the baby were. "I've been her owner for like a few weeks."

"So fucking what?" I frowned. "It's all I can think about with Ava. If she gets through the next month without getting knocked up, it won't be for want of trying."

"Ava?" The voice from the back said. How had I forgotten they were from the same community?

"Yes," I said. "Ava from Sanctuary. You can see her soon."

"They're not supposed to have any contact for a month," Carter said.

I raised a brow. He gave me the what-the-fuck look.

"I want to see her now," Nora said with a note of demand.

"Babe, you're not supposed to have contact for a month," Carter repeated, sounding tired.

"A month! And you didn't think to mention that your brother was her owner... and hell-bent on impregnating her?"

"Can we talk about this later?" Carter said 'later' like it was a not very subtle code word for never.

My lips twitched at their little domestic spat. Carter had struggled to adapt when we first arrived in Taylor's world. He'd been tough before, he'd had to be, but I wanted something better for him. There were twelve years between us, but he was my blood, the only blood I had left in the world. I'd told him to knuckle down when the tests revealed his intelligence, and he'd done exactly that. On reflection, at the expense of living.

I thought Nora might be good for him, kid and all.

My perspectives had changed since a certain wildcat had entered my life.

"At least tell me if she's okay," Nora said. "She went out to get the meds for Adam. We didn't see her for three days, and then Sanctuary fell. I'd feared the worst. She's not exactly street-savvy, not without Jodi."

"Don't mention that crazy bitch to me," I muttered before I could think better. "She's already chewed my ear out and issued a challenge for Ava."

Nora chuckled. "Yes, that would be Jodi," she said. "They've been together for a long time."

"Blaine found Ava near Sanctuary," Carter said. He reached his hand back between the seats. "I treated her after. She was fine, a little dehydrated, but fine considering she was on the streets."

"I'm glad," she said. "I'm so glad. She'll be excited when she finds out about Adam. She loves him very much. Used to call him her honorary nephew."

As I pulled into the underground garage, I realized I would need to tell Ava about Nora and my brother. It was clear that the two women were close. Minds greater than mine had determined that new arrivals could not make contact with former associates for a month. It was supposed to help them settle into their new situation quicker. I'd had no first-hand experience with it before, but now it felt cold and cruel.

As I pulled up into my space and switched the engine off, I stopped to hold a look with Carter. "You going to be okay?"

"Yeah." He nodded. "Feel a little rough. I've felt worse."

I let them leave first, watching the way he drew her into his arm as they waited for the elevator to arrive. I still thought of him as a kid, which was ridiculous since he'd grown up the hard way when society took a turn for the worse.

And now here he was with a family of his own.

Which brought me back to a frustrating conversation with Ava's former girlfriend, and psycho bitch, Jodi. She had decked me this morning. Not a word passed her lips as she marched up to me and punched me in the jaw.

I can't even lie to myself and claim it didn't hurt. She reeled off a bunch of demands but eventually had calmed enough for us to have a conversation. She had been cagey, but it was clear there were things about Ava's past that I needed to know.

With a sigh, I hopped out of the vehicle and headed on up.

Ava

I'd got a message from Blaine to say that tomorrow I would be allowed out. I greeted this news with a measure of excitement and trepidation. Yes, I wanted to escape the luxurious confinement of his apartment, the monotony of which was broken only by the arrival of his sweet cleaner or Blaine himself. But I was also nervous about this new community and how I would fit in.

He looked tired when he entered the apartment still in his combat kit. Usually, he cleaned up somewhere before returning. Today, he was a mess, reminding me of the life he led when he exited the door. With a brief lift of his hand, he headed into the bedroom en-suite. The sounds of the shower followed.

I hung back in the lounge, my stomach fluttering with the anticipation of him being inside me once again. Would this feeling between us ever change? Was it merely the newness of our relationship that made us turn to each other the moment he arrived and throughout the night?

I didn't know. But I thought I was on the way to becoming addicted to the sweet escape I found when he was near.

When he returned to the lounge, he was dressed in a pair of loose sweatpants that hung low on his hips to reveal that arresting, finely sculptured upper body, along with the enticing V at his hips. It didn't get any easier to be around him. The man was stunning in every way. He caught hold of my hips as he sat back on the couch, drawing me onto his lap with my knees to either side of his slim hips so that my pussy nestled close to that tempting bulge.

"Someone spent a lot of money on your enhancements," he said, brushing the hair back from my face, I was sure, so that he could see any tells. "And no ownership mark? How did you manage to avoid that?"

So, that was where this was going. I wondered if he'd spoken to Jodi. She wouldn't offer up my secrets easily... unless she thought it were necessary.

Did she think Blaine needed to know?

I wished I could see her. She was always better at reading places and people than me. Only I wasn't with Jodi anymore. I was with Blaine, and I had no idea how it might feel when I saw her again.

"I lived far from the cities for a while," I said. Removing the guardian tattoo had been a particularly dark moment. Without the use of a brander, that had meant cutting the skin away. Thankfully, my enhancements had prevented an infection. The skin had healed back flawlessly, like it had never been there.

I kept my lashes lowered, but I could feel Blaine's silent study. He'd put me here on his lap, facing him in this vulnerable position for a reason.

"You expect me to believe that? What's your real name?"

"My real name is not important." I'd known this would come at some point, the questions about the lack of brand. My luminous eyes... "Would you rather I made something up?"

His laughter sounded cold. "I've been inside you every way a man can, but you still don't fucking trust me."

When I met his eyes, I found his expression indiscernible.

That flutter was back again, the determination that I could and should trust him. Yet, trust was so hard.

"I can't help you or protect you from whatever it is that you're running from if you don't let me in," he said softly.

My chest felt tight. I wanted to tell him; wanted to get off the ride. "You can't protect me from this," I replied.

"Try me," he said with bite, eyes glittering.

No one, and especially a man like Blaine, wanted to hear that they were inadequate, but it was so much bigger than he could possibly imagine or understand. I could neither run nor hide forever.

I was on borrowed time here, I knew that.

Like Sanctuary had been.

I thought Guilder City might be more fleeting as options went. My uncle had contacts here. In Blaine's own words, I was a woman who drew attention. Perhaps, word of the woman with the unusual eyes had already spread. My uncle was a man of resources. He would never stop looking for me because that was the kind of person he was. Perhaps, someone at the hospital had provided a tip-off to one of his minions. Perhaps, Blaine's innocent cleaner. Sanctuary had kept Jodi and me off the radar. Guilder City had the potential to thrust us back into the spotlight.

"Kiss me," he said. "The kind of kiss that will make me forget all the secrets you're keeping."

My pulse picked up, throbbing at the base of my throat. Dark lust and burning need hit me: mine, his, and a potent combination of them both.

"I won't ask you again."

He wanted the answers that I wasn't providing and needed to claw back some control. Yet, there was an allure in being defiant. As much as he needed my submission, I needed a distraction from the voices clamoring in my head.

I wanted him out of control, and his face told me that he was heading there fast.

His grin had a feral edge. He was a dangerous man, and I thought that was a large part of his appeal. He would oblige my desire for oblivion.

"There's a part of me that says I should give you what you want," he said. "And so decisively that you're too afraid to make the same mistake again. But there's also another side of me that fucking hates manipulation and says I should do the exact opposite."

He grinned, and I suffered a belated determination that I'd bitten off more than I could chew.

"You know, I think I'm just going to make a call on this on an entirely selfish basis."

He stood, lifting me with him, and I clung lest I fall.

"Let's take this to the bedroom," he said. "Going to need lots of lube for what I've got in mind."

Chapter Nineteen

Nora

I existed in a state of turmoil as we entered the apartment. I'd been through a rollercoaster of emotion, and the day was not done with me yet.

Adam was a little fussy. It was time for his dinner, but he was not the highest priority in my life for once. I felt sick, my tummy all in knots and my thoughts looping over that horrific scene in the medical center garage.

"Do you need some ice?"

I could have slapped myself for that stupid question. Of course he needed ice... a ton of painkillers, and probably a few stitches given he was still bleeding at his temple.

"I'll get it," Carter said, not meeting my eyes. "Adam needs his dinner."

I burst out crying. Adam burst out crying.

Carter took Adam from me while I fell apart. Wrapping an arm around my waist, he guided me over to the couch.

"I need to get you some ice!" I wailed.

"Five minutes won't make a difference one way or the other," he said.

"How can you be so calm?"

"I'm not going to die, babe." I went to pull away, but he refused to let go, and all my struggles did was plaster me up against him tighter. Adam's tears turned to giggles as he thumped the side of Carter's face. "Need to work on that right hook, buddy."

I snorted out a laugh, and although tears still dampened my cheeks, I could feel Carter's calm invading me. "Let me hold him so he doesn't hurt you."

"Nope, I like feeling you next to me. I *need* to feel you next to me."

I forced my breathing to be steady, took in the way he was so gentle with Adam and with me, and wondered how the hell I'd happened upon this miracle. With my cheek against his chest, I breathed in his scent, taking comfort from his steady heartbeat under my ear. I wanted to stay in this moment forever, to enjoy this awareness growing between us.

Adam started to fidget. The little warning warbles that said he was overtired, possibly needed his diaper changed and food. "Let me see to him... and get you some ice. Please."

He let me take Adam this time. With Adam on my hip, I grabbed a prepared meal for him from the fridge and put it on the side with his spoon, ready to go. Then I took some ice and wrapped it in a towel.

Carter took the ice from me, wincing as he pressed it to his temple. I couldn't look at his poor face without wanting to cry again.

I sucked it up and carried Adam through to his room where I changed his diaper. The apartment had a small dining table opposite the couch, where I sat with Adam in his new highchair.

He ate the food like he'd been starved, chubby baby fists waving enthusiastically.

I went through the motions of feeding him, bathing him, and putting him to bed. In the background, I heard Carter take a shower and go to bed without bothering to eat.

My tension rose as I showered and donned one of Carter's old T-shirts he'd given me for bed. The soft cotton that was usually pleasant against my skin felt tight and restrictive. My breasts, the bane of my adult life, felt heavy and achy.

When I entered the bedroom, I found Carter sitting at the end of the bed, sleep pants low on his hips. The bedside lamp cast a weak illumination over him. Bruises covered his chest and across his ribs. Seeing it broke my heart.

God help me, I did not know how to do any of this.

He took my hand, drawing me between the V of his open legs.

"Babe, you need to tell me if someone approaches you like that again."

"Okay." I knew that. My reluctance in telling him about the man confused even me. Maybe I'd been fooled into the civilized front Guilder City presented and thought I was safe?

"If it happens again, you need to tell me straight away. You have the cell, you can message me. No matter how small the interest is. I can handle a challenge, but I can't handle the 'off-the-grid' kind of bullshit that happened tonight. Do you realize what would have happened had Blaine not turned up?"

I swallowed. Yes, it had dawned upon me that something was very wrong with the way we'd been approached in the garage. The significance hadn't registered fully until his brother, Blaine, had arrived and called them on the corrupt challenge.

Blaine, who was with Ava.

Blaine, who looked capable of taking on all ten of the thugs single-handed and not breaking a sweat. Not that Carter was a lightweight.

My throat turned to dust as I remembered Carter leaning over the fallen man, fists laying blow after blow, the blood splattering, and the plaintive cries of the downed man.

I'd never seen a man fight like that before. If Blaine hadn't stepped in and dragged him off, I thought Carter might have killed the man from bed 17E.

Glenn—how I'd loved him—but he was a gentle soul and was no better equipped than me for this fallen world.

But Carter, the man I'd thought of as young and weak, had destroyed a street-hardy pimp.

My eyes went to the hand holding mine, and I became enrapt by the scuffed, bruised knuckles.

"We good?" he asked.

"Yes." I stepped into him, drawing his head against my stomach and stroking fingers through his silken hair.

With a deep breath, he pressed his face into me, hands closing over the back of my thighs and sliding up until they cupped my naked ass. Everything inside me came alive, my stomach dipped, and my legs grew weak.

"I can't be gentle, Nora," he said. "Not tonight, not now. I'm so fucking pumped."

My pussy clenched in anticipation. "It's okay. I don't want gentle tonight either. I just want to forget."

My T-shirt was tugged over my head, and I was tossed to the bed. I expected him to climb over me, to fuck me, but I caught only a wicked grin before he lowered his lips to my breast and sucked my nipple—hard.

I went a little insane under his attention. He was rough with me. Rough in a way that spoke of barely contained desire. His fingers shook as they squeezed my breasts together, nipping and kissing with enough force that I knew it would leave marks.

It made me hot and impatient. It sent me a little wild.

Then he worked his way down my stomach, and my breath caught as he parted the slick lips of my pussy and dived in like he was starved.

"Oh!" My legs tried and failed to close. It was too intense and too much. The sum of my life sexual encounters were the rushed, fumbled couplings with Glenn that were more about connection than pleasure and the brutality that came after he died. I'd forced myself to forget both for different reasons. But my life had no context to draw on for this witchcraft Carter performed on my body.

Then his tongue found my clit, and I nearly levitated off the bed. A high, urgent coil was twisting me up and up. I thought this must be the pinnacle of pleasure until he caught the hot needy little nub between his lips and gently sucked.

Oh. My. God.

If Adam woke, I was going to lose my mind.

Carter stopped.

Why had he stopped?

What torturous trick was this?

"You're tensing up, babe."

I blinked at him in confusion.

"I was thinking about Adam." The rest was better left undisclosed.

He scrubbed at his jaw and appeared genuinely bemused. "I must be doing something wrong."

What? "God, no." I shook my head. My entire pussy was tingling; my clit was throbbing. I needed him to finish what he'd started. "I was worried he might wake up."

Smirking, and much to my disappointment, he shifted back.

But then he put me on my hands and knees, kicked off his sleep pants, and filled me in a single thrust.

It hurt. It hurt a lot. I'd had a baby, for goodness sake, but no one had been inside me since long before Adam was born, and he was nearly nine months old. I couldn't see what Carter was packing, but I felt every glorious inch.

"Fuck, babe, you've taken it all," he muttered. I was still reeling from this statement when he pulled back and plowed me again.

"Fuck, yes." Hands bracing my hips, he took me roughly and I loved every brutal moment. I came alive for him in a way I'd never done before. My body sawed on and off his cock, breasts swaying, ass slapping against him with every savage thrust. I pushed back, welcoming the ache deep inside, trembling with the strain of bracing myself.

"I'm going to fill this perfect pussy up."

Those growled words were like a shot of raw lust that sent my pussy clenching and throbbing in joy.

"You like the sound of that, babe?"

"Yes!"

A fist tightened over my hair, arching my head back, and I swear I was close to coming apart.

"I might get you pregnant, Nora."

I whimpered, delirious with how good that sounded.

"Tell me to fill you up." A savage thrust was followed by the grinding of his crotch against my ass like he was trying to force it even deeper. "Tell me!"

"Please, I need you to come inside me. Please, come inside. I need it so bad."

I wanted him bound to me.

Wanted the man who was gentle with Adam and me.

Wanted the monster who could fight.

And I wanted the rough lover who was using me just right.

I wanted everything he had to offer. I wanted it all.

151

Adrenaline flooded, a sweet ache deep inside that tipped into blissful contractions over his thick heavenly cock.

I swear he was deep enough to find my soul when he slammed and held.

His warmth flooded me.

My pussy fluttered in the aftermath, greedily sucking his seed into my womb where I needed it most.

We reached for each other so many times during the night. For the first time since I'd arrived at Carter's apartment, Adam didn't wake.

But the morning brought a message on Carter's cell, and from the way he tensed, I knew it wasn't the good kind of news. An important announcement that we must attend, I was told, with the man who called himself king.

I didn't want to go. I wanted to hide in the bed and never leave the room again.

One thing I'd learned about Carter in the short time since I'd known him was that he was patient.

He took the time to explain to me why this was important.

One thing I'd learned about myself is that I was as stubborn as a proverbial mule when I decided I either did or didn't want to do something. His explanations sounded reasonable, but I still didn't want to go, a deep in the pit of my gut aversion. I came up with an impressive cast of reasons why Adam and I should stay at home. Really, my inventiveness knew no bounds.

Another thing I'd learned about Carter during our short acquaintance was that he didn't tolerate any bullshit, which was very fucking frustrating. When he started that stern count-down, I knew I'd lost this round.

Chapter Twenty

Carter

The next day, I could have used a break.

No one got a break in Guilder City.

A call came informing me that Taylor was making an announcement, which meant that I, along with around three thousand other personnel, were expected to attend.

I felt like shit and wasn't in the mood to hear about his next expansion plan. We were still dealing with the fallout from the last big push that had delivered the self-appointed king another city. Injury rates were still high, and the territory was far from fully assimilated.

"Why do I need to go?" Nora demanded.

The threat of repercussion and my countdown had got her ass out of bed and in the shower, but she was still radiating feistiness as she paced back and forth before where I sat on the end of the bed, bouncing Adam in her arms.

"This isn't a democracy," I said, shoving my right foot into my boot and yanking the laces tight. "When Taylor addresses, attendance is mandatory. They don't give out apartments like this to everyone. I made myself useful after I arrived. Went through the basic medical training before specializing in genetics." I shoved my left foot into my boot and tightened the laces up. "You make yourself useful to Taylor, and he will look after you. So, yeah, I attend these things. That way, when Adam needs some new stuff, it appears as if by magic. I own you now. That means if I attend, so do you."

Ownership. It still set a strange heat low in my belly whenever I acknowledged it.

It brought out a territorial side of me I'd never experienced before.

I'd marked her body up, first with the brander, and then in a primitive way: faint bruises where my fingers had braced her hips, love bites on her throat, tits, and inner thighs. I thought I ought to be more conflicted about my need to mark her perfect skin. She hadn't been conflicted though, she had encouraged me, coming apart on a scream that I'd had to smother with my hand when I sucked with particular savagery against her throat.

As I'd run my fingertips over the marks in the early hours of the morning, I'd felt only satisfaction and pride.

When I glanced up, she still had a mulish set to her jaw. So much for me seeing the softer side after the fuck-fest last night. I just wanted to toss her on the bed and fuck the stubborn right out of her.

Unfortunately, there wasn't time.

But there was always tonight.

I knew the grin spreading across my face had a feral edge. If Nora kept up this whining, she would find out what happened when I got to *one*.

"What?" She frowned faintly, which only made my smirk broader.

I stood. Wide blue eyes blinked up at me then lowered

when I adjusted my dick in my pants, failing to find a position that didn't exacerbate the hard-on.

Her pretty, pink cupid-bow lips formed an O before she hustled her ass out of the bedroom like it was on fire.

I followed her into the lounge.

"What's he like? Taylor? Will I be expected to talk to him?"

I smiled, humoring her distraction. "No, it's too big for that. Usually several thousand people attend. And yes, they check attendees." My smile faded. "It's not perfect here, Nora. I'll be honest, I don't know what perfect is. Just stories Blaine has told me over the years. Taylor isn't the worst out there, that much I know. He accepts differing opinions, might even be open to suggestions from time to time. But when he decides something or mandates something, it's final. He's fair to those who follow the rules and ruthless to those who don't. And when I say ruthless, he will kill anyone who causes dissent."

The buzzer drew our attention.

Nora

I'd been expecting Ava. I wasn't expecting Mary and Rachel. I burst out crying, which Adam was none too pleased about.

"They allocated us together," Mary said, answering my question. Rachel beamed as she spotted her honorary little brother.

"Is he well now?" the little girl asked earnestly. "They said he'd been treated at the hospital."

"Yes, sweetheart, he's all better now. I've missed you guys so much." I opened my arm in an invitation, and she came straight over for a hug with Adam and me. "How have you both been?" I glanced up at Mary with a smile as I handed Adam over to a giggling Rachel.

Adam was making his happy baby noises and clearly excited by the arrival of his familiar play partner.

Mary's smile was wry. "We're doing fine, honey." She glanced around the apartment with interest. "Not doing as good as you." She winked. "But the place they gave us is clean, and we're near a couple of Sanctuary folks." She rattled off the name of a few of the older ladies who'd lived within Sanctuary.

"Do you—" I suddenly felt very awkward in wanting to ask but was nevertheless curious. "Do you have an owner?"

Mary made a little snorting noise.

Rachel giggled again. "She's got a suitor!"

My brows raised, and a smile bloomed. "A suitor?"

"Huff. Us older women past childbearing age, don't need an owner." She glared without heat at Rachel, who still laughed. "But we're expected to accept suitors. Why some old crusty has-been wants companionship, I can't say. I told him straight to put the radio on if he wants to listen to folk talking nonsense. Fool seemed to think I was being funny."

"A suitor with a mind to becoming your owner?" I asked to be absolutely sure. I couldn't imagine Mary with any man, yet I got a strong impression that she wasn't immune to her suitor's charms. I was also ashamed to admit that I'd been too caught up in my own woes to think through how ownership might work for the older women. I was delighted to hear that it wasn't forced upon them in the same way. I thought it shouldn't be forced upon anyone, but any concession felt worthy of celebration. It wasn't perfect here, Carter had said as much, but it wasn't terrible either. And I was delighted to find that Rachel had been allowed to stay with Mary.

"So he keeps telling me," Mary scoffed with a roll of her eyes. Then her face softened. "But enough about me. You know you scared us witless when you marched up to that soldier and demanded someone treat your baby."

"I wasn't thinking straight." I mentally winced, wondering at my crazy. But I'd been so worried about Adam that the risks were unimportant. "It worked out. It's such a relief to see him well and know it's forever."

"Adam's not the only one who's looking better," Mary said, boney fingers closing over my hand in a tight squeeze. "You deserve a break," she whispered for my ears only. "Hell, we all do." Leaning back, she placed her hand against my cheek. "The only constant in this life is change. Don't always know if it's the good kind or the bad kind. Can't hide from it, and sure as hell can't stop it. Can only buckle up and get ready for the ride. Don't talk about the past much, and that's for the best if you ask me. We all got our share of hurting. From the looks of the sweet guy eyeing us with concern, I'd say you found one of the rare good ones."

I nodded, feeling the sentiments of her words to my very core. There'd been so many bumps since I'd first met Carter. I'd been super rude to him in the hospital. The next day I'd claimed he'd offered to be my owner. Then he *had* become my owner. He was complex. I'd seen the scars on his body, along with the new ones he'd acquired defending me. I'd barely scratched the surface of knowing him, but everything I'd seen had shown me what a good man he was. Mary was right. We didn't talk about the past for a good reason. But I'd still spent too much time wallowing in memories. It was time to put my past life to bed, both the fleeting good parts and the darkness.

I smiled, my eyes instinctively going to Carter. "Yeah, I really did."

Ava

Blaine was barely home, and when he *was* home, he damn near killed me with his attention. But I couldn't lay all the blame at his door; I was a willing and equal participant.

Then there was his reaction to Jodi that had shown me another side to him. I was more convinced than ever that I was in love with him, which would make it even harder when I was forced to leave.

News of an announcement that I must attend brought my days living in a bubble to an end. Something had happened last night, and Blaine had been cagey ever since.

So, here I was, dressed up in a new outfit with jeans, boots, and even a new hooded jacket that was warm and soft to the touch. It had been a long time since I'd had new things.

I could get used to this, whatever this was.

But I shouldn't because that would only make it hurt worse.

Leaving the apartment was surreal enough, standing beside him in the elevator more so. How things had changed since I'd last stood here with him. Back then, I'd been a terrified, nervous wreck, exhausted from my days on the streets and wondering at my fate.

I was still wondering about my fate, but now it was a different story, and I no longer feared the man.

He didn't hit the ground floor button as I expected; instead, he selected a floor. I turned to study his profile. Leaving home after so many days was weird enough; this was even weirder. "I thought we needed to drive there?"

"We do." His lips tugged up on one side, and he winked at me. "But we're stopping off on the way."

Okay, I guess I would find out what this was about when he was good and ready.

The floor we stopped at had notably more doors leading

off each side than the one where Blaine's apartment was. Taking my hand in his, he led me to the end of a long passage where he stopped at an indistinct door. He glanced down at me with an expression that was hard to interpret. "My younger brother lives here," he said before pressing his finger to the buzzer.

He was so cryptic that I'd no idea what to expect.

It definitely wasn't the young doctor who'd tended to me when I first arrived. I blinked a couple of times. He was dressed casually in jeans and a T-shirt, which threw me... as did the cuts and bruises on his face.

Had he been in a fight?

My head turned from one man to another. How had I not noticed the similarities last time? In my defense, I'd been a little woozy post-adventure on the streets. Carter was younger by a significant amount, but the likeness was there.

"Is that Ava?"

Carter stepped aside, and the new faces that came into view had me reeling back on my heels.

I barely noticed Blaine urging me inside and the door closing; my focus was all on the woman and the little boy I'd wondered if I would ever see again. Nora and Adam were not the only two faces greeting me; Mary and Rachel were also here.

"It's so good to see you all! Nora, how is Adam?" I hugged everyone, even Mary, who was not much of a hugger. Rachel loved cuddles and was eager for her turn. Poor Adam garbled his complaint, having no idea what his crazy Aunty Ava was all about. Rachel offered Adam to me for a cuddle. She had always been so good with the little boy.

"He's doing great," Nora said, pretty face turning blotchy as she wiped away tears. "He—Carter performed a procedure on him when we first arrived. Adam is cured."

I hugged Adam tightly while he made his little baby gurgles and gripped my hair like a lifeline.

Rachel laughed. "I think he missed you," she said.

"Yeah, you miss me, Adam?" I rubbed his back and drew his comforting baby scent in. He was clinging to me just as tightly, head pressed into the nook of my shoulder and arms wrapped like he was never going to let go. I'd always wondered how much babies understood. God, I'd missed them so much.

"What on earth are you doing here?" I turned slightly to glance over Adam's head at the two men watching us with intense expressions. "In Carter's home?"

"I'm—um." Her face flushed bright red, and her eyes shot toward Carter.

"She's got an owner," Rachel piped up.

"Oh!" I said, noticing the new mark at Nora's temple... and was that a hickey on her throat? She had always made a point of covering up the ugly tattoo her former owner had branded her with. For the first time, I could remember, her gorgeous red hair was tied back into a ponytail allowing the new ownership brand to peep through.

Nora, who hated men with a passion, was with a man, not just any man, but a handsome doctor who had to be at least five years younger. I bit my lip to try and stifle my smile.

"What?" she demanded. And right there was the feisty woman I knew and loved.

I grinned openly.

"You have no reason to judge," she said with meaning, but her eyes held a spark of mischief that she showed so rarely.

She looked good—healthy, but there was also something else that made me think of a soul-deep kind of wellness that had been missing.

And she was right; I had no right to judge. I could see she had questions. Most people within the community of Sanctuary had questions about Jodi and me. Most assumed we were together, and we had been for a while. But what we felt had transitioned from one type of love to another.

"I've spoken to Jodi," I said, reaching over to take Nora's hand and squeeze it gently.

"Don't mention that crazy bitch," Blaine said with meaning. I threw a scowl at him over my shoulder, although it held no more heat than his comment, and I found myself smiling at him instead. His eyes dropped to Adam, who was still clinging in a way that I thought might be edging toward sleep.

I knew what Blaine was thinking. He'd made it clear he wanted a child with me. He damn near broke me with his enthusiasm for precisely that. I should be relieved that it hadn't happened yet—my life was complicated enough.

I wasn't relieved. The thought of staying here and having Blaine's child filled my heart with joy.

I looked away, fearing my emotions were too close to the surface.

Blaine

Ava was hiding something. I was more convinced than ever. I wanted to drag her straight back to my apartment and force her to tell me what the hell was going on by fair means or foul. By the time I was done, her ass would be glowing red, and she would get fucked within an inch of her life.

The second part wasn't much of a stretch; I was pounding her pussy every chance I got.

"We need to leave," Carter said, glancing at his watch.

Ava passed the kid back to the little girl. Seeing Ava hold the baby had stirred up the primitive in me. I wanted to watch her belly grow, wanted to see her holding our child in the same loving way, but I also wanted her thoroughly claimed and bound to me in every way I could.

Earlier, Jodi had offered a smug grin as she told me that Ava wasn't for me.

It had riled me; I could admit this. Ava and I were still too new to one another, still trying to navigate a relationship while I was only partially present and making questionable use of the time we *were* together.

Later, I promised myself we would have that chat.

Chapter Twenty-One

Ava

Leaving Adam with Mary and Rachel, we took Blaine's Humvee together.

Today, I got my first real view of Guilder City in daylight. For once, it wasn't raining, and my eyes often strayed from Nora to the world beyond the window. We sat together in the back of the Humvee, Blaine and Carter in the front.

"I can't believe you've been in the same apartment building the whole time," I said, feeling a happy grin spread across my face. The more time I spent with Nora, the more I could see how she was blooming into this new life.

"Me neither," she said. The narrowing of her eyes suggested Carter would be in for a hard time. Yes, and so would Blaine. I understood we were not supposed to have any contact for a month... for whatever stupid reasons they had, but it still felt unnecessary.

Nora chatted about her work at the hospital, about the day care there, and the other staff. For as long as I'd known Nora, she had struggled with her health. Bouts of lethargy, headaches, body aches, and pains that she battled with daily both before and after Adam was born. I knew she had been hurt badly during her time on the streets before Jodi picked her up.

The rule said you didn't talk about your past. There were times when I'd clung to that rule, but now I thought it was stupid. Perhaps, had I been a better friend, I might have asked Nora about her past.

Might even have shared some of mine. And maybe it might have helped us both heal a little.

It was too late to fix the past, but I was hopeful about tomorrow.

Our conversation died as we pulled into the complex that I thought might have been a conference facility in that bygone time. The Humvee slowed as it entered the parking garage beneath. Unlike the one at the apartment, this one was well lit and full of other cars. Two soldiers were stationed inside the entrance, and they directed us to a space.

"Perfect timing," Carter said as the vehicle rolled to a stop. "You want Ava to stay with Nora and me?"

"Yeah, probably for the best," Blaine replied, glancing back over his shoulder at me. "I'm less bothered about Taylor than his nosy-assed minions. Don't want to end up in a challenge on her first day out. Not that any of Taylor's advisors have a chance, but they have paid muscle they could call on to piss me off."

My stomach turned over—way to crank up my tension.

His lips tugged up in a grin. "Don't worry, baby. They won't win. I just don't want to give Carter any extra work fixing them up."

Opening the door, he hopped down.

Carter muttered, "Asshole!" Before he did the same.

The door beside me opened, and Blaine closed his hands around my waist to help me down.

"You going to be okay with Carter and Nora?"

I nodded.

Leaning in, he took my lips in a swift kiss.

I was so damn deep into this man.

Then he was drawing me out of the way and slamming the door shut. "Taylor will expect me to be with him. I'll come find you after."

He left, heading up the stairs we'd parked near at a jog, while I followed behind with Carter and Nora.

Guards with automatic weapons were stationed at the entrance. They vetted Carter via a scan of his brand, repeating for Nora and me. Inside, I found a vast, softly lit auditorium, close to capacity.

We took our seats near the back as the doors closed and the lights dimmed, illuminating a low dais.

I knew instantly that the man standing there was Taylor, the self-proclaimed king.

Standing right beside him was Blaine.

The speech went over my head. I was so distracted by Blaine's presence on the stage. My first venture beyond his apartment had offered a plethora of revelations.

Sitting here, one might imagine the collapse had never happened. On the surface, it was civilized. A select crowd gathered, attentively listening to their leader talk through the changes that were happening within the community.

It wasn't normal, though, and a sense of discord enveloped me. The man on the podium was a dictator. None of us had a choice in what happened to us or any aspect of our future. I remembered my parents bemoaning politics before civilization imploded. The saying, *power corrupts, and absolute power corrupts absolutely* was manifested in the man who held our enrapt attention. It wasn't terrible here, but it wasn't a democracy, and nothing suggested it would change for the better soon.

Blaine's place of prominence within this kingdom remained the biggest shock. I'd realized his luxurious home spoke of more than a soldier, but not to this extent. As Taylor finished, Blaine gave an update on the operation that had handed Sanctuary, and the surrounding city, to the king.

There was safety in the arms of a man who wielded his own brand of power.

But was there enough?

My mind turned, as it was wont to do at weak moments, back to my uncle's community. Martin had taken my mother as a partner after my father died.

His brother—my father—dead because Martin had killed him.

And the monster wanted me.

While there, I'd been living under a cloud of desperation, watching my mother fade, and knowing the only thing that kept her going was the knowledge that she was shielding me.

And then he'd killed her.

My hands were shaking. I wrapped them around my waist and fought to bring my mounting horror down.

I blamed myself. Hated that I'd watched on while Martin destroyed her. Hated that I hadn't been able to do anything to help. But I mostly hated that if I'd dared to go to him, he might have freed her from this terrible fate, and she might still live.

I was weak, selfish, and a fool.

I missed my mother so much.

I missed my father, who was different from Martin in every way.

My focus returned to the proceedings. The king was once more speaking about a new alliance in negotiation. Then he was welcoming his new dictator buddy to the stage.

I blinked, sure that my memories had conjured the man who rose from the front to join Taylor from the darkest recess of my mind.

Cold sweat popped across my skin. He'd aged a little, but not enough for me to be confused.

It was him.

My tormentor and my uncle.

The man who had killed my father.

Who had also killed my mother... the catalyst for me finally fleeing with Jodi that fateful night.

And he was now standing beside Blaine.

I'd never been one for second-guessing myself. If life had taught me anything, it was that at times you needed to act and act fast. Inside, I felt sick with fear, but outside, I was cold and determined.

Blaine would be furious with Carter, and I felt bad about that, but not enough to deter me. My hands shook as I gave my excuses, grateful that no one accompanied me. Despite my best attempts to keep my expectations realistic, a part of me had died realizing that I must leave.

I'd been so close to trusting Blaine.

How could I have been so stupid?

Fleeing the conference center was easier than I thought. Head down, hood up; security was more concerned with those seeking entrance than leaving.

My uncle had fitted me with a tracker, and I'd already checked and found one under Blaine's brand.

That went first.

I'd hacked into Blaine's datapad days ago and had installed a hotkey combination on my cell that would redirect the tracking location to Blaine's cell. It would have been better to cut the brand out altogether, but I didn't have a knife nor the nerve to try and hack into my skin to remove it.

The redirection would be sufficient for now. I had bigger problems to deal with.

My cell was my only point of contention. In the end, I erred on the side of caution and tossed it.

A bonus was the proximity of the river. It had been years since I'd swam, but it would be the fastest way to remove myself from the area. After a few minutes of assessing the tide via the floating rubbish, I could see it was incoming.

Not for the first time, I thanked my genetics as I slipped into the filthy water, letting it carry me for a distance before striking out for the far shore.

I was shivering by the time I heaved myself onto the muddy bank. Scrubby, stunted, leafless trees lined this side of the river, tangled with plastic, tattered rags, and other refuse. Setting off at a brisk pace, my only thought was to get as far away from Taylor and my uncle as was possible before exhaustion took me.

So I walked.

Tomorrow, I would work out where I was and figure out how to get to a rendezvous point agreed with Jodi.

Chapter Twenty-Two

Blaine

When Taylor's update was finally over, there were a dozen messages on my cell.

All of them were from Carter.

I hit dial even as I was jogging along the corridor that circled the auditorium, the mother of all bad feelings roiling in my gut.

"She's gone," he said as the call connected, and I swear the blood drained in a flash before surging right back.

"The fuck are you talking about?" I growled into the cell. "Where are you now?"

I reached them a few minutes later. The main room had dispersed into clusters as the select crowd was given leave to mingle. Carter and Nora were waiting in the corridor outside the main entrance, soldiers beside them on their communicators and looking shifty as hell when I stormed up.

"Where the fuck is she?"

"We don't know," Carter said. "She said she felt sick and went to the bathroom, maybe thirty minutes ago. We didn't realize anything was off at first."

"She can't be that far away." I pulled up the tracking app on my cell. Her first fucking time out of the apartment, and she had run. I couldn't see her getting far, given she was fitted with a tracker, but her attempt still pissed me off.

The notion that she had been playing me sat like lead in my gut.

Had she left with Jodi? I fucking owned her. She didn't get to walk away.

It took a few seconds for me to assimilate the data on the app. The little green dot was right here. "What the hell is happening?"

"Hey, guy with the dick and very little else!" As I looked up, I copped a fist in my face.

I rocked back on my heels. The nearby soldiers waded in to drag Jodi off, which was for the best because I was going to knock her out cold if she came at me again.

"You crazy fucking bitch. Where is she?"

She fought the soldiers. "Where is she? What the fuck is wrong with you?" she roared at me. "You were supposed to be protecting her. Not cozying up with her fucking psycho uncle."

My brows pinched together as I tried to piece together this minefield and failed.

Mitch rounded the corner at a jog as I was about to take Jodi by the throat.

"The fuck, Jodi?" Mitch said. "You promised you wouldn't start anything. You gave me your fucking word!"

The fight went out of her—it went out of me too—and the soldiers released her cautiously. "You got my word right up until golden boy here started schmoozing with Ava's sick uncle."

"Who the fuck is her uncle?" I demanded. Not Taylor? He'd never once mentioned a missing niece.

"She never told you, did she?" Jodi's smug face set my teeth on edge. If Mitch hadn't waded in, I'd have decked the bitch for sure.

"She's missing," I said. "Her tracker isn't working. Tell me what I need to fucking know!"

Her smirk dropped, and she looked so fucking ill that it brought a surge of near debilitating fear.

"The man on the stage with Taylor," she spat. "Martin Zander is her uncle. He killed her father soon after the collapse. Took her mother as his partner. He didn't want her mother—he wanted Ava. She wouldn't leave. Not while her mother was trapped there with him. I was Ava's bodyguard." Her voice softened to a growl. "Zander killed her mother and told Ava it was time she took her rightful place. We fled the same night. I cut his brand from her temple myself."

Her chest was heaving. She wasn't lying; I could see the terrible truth in every strained line of her face.

"She's got hacking skills," she said, voice lowering. "It's the only reason we got out. Whatever you think you have to track her, she'll know how to disable it. She has probably redirected it to someone else. Knowing Ava, she's had a contingency plan for a while. This community was always too big for her to be safe. But when she said she wanted to stay with you, I fucking hoped I was wrong."

"Okay," Mitch said. "The tracker is still inside her, which means we can restore whatever she did."

"You think Zander didn't try to do the same and failed?" Jodi said.

"Yeah, well, we have ten times the resources Zander does," Mitch said. "So I'm going to give it a shot."

I nodded. Mitch moved to the side and got straight on his communicator.

"Do you have any idea where she might go?" I asked Jodi.

She shrugged. "She's not safe while he's alive. She won't stay here now that Taylor is associating with Zander. Even if you find her, she'll run again."

"Why wouldn't she have told me instead of running?" I swiped a hand down my face.

"Are you fucking dumb?" Jodi asked, face twisting in a sneer. "What are you going to do if Taylor asks you to hand her over as part of his new deal with Zander? You going to say no to your king?"

"You're damn right I'm going to say no," I bit back.

"It wouldn't matter to Zander," she said. "Once Zander finds out she's here, he'll break the alliance in a flash for what he wants. He's fucking obsessed with her."

"Zander is that much of a threat to her?"

"Yeah, he's a threat," Jodi said. "She'll never be safe while that asshole lives."

"Blaine?" The soft warning in Carter's voice barely registered. "Don't do something stupid."

"Hell yeah," Jodi goaded. "Do something stupid. I'll hold your fucking hand while you do it. You going to kill him?"

I pinned her with a look. My eyes shifted toward Mitch, who was off his communicator and giving me a cagy look. "Keep working on her tracker," I said, stabbing a finger at him. "I'll be back once I've eliminated the threat."

"Are you going to kill him?" Jodi demanded. Damn, the bitch was pushy.

I nodded. She was hiding something. "Something I need to know?"

She folded her arms. "Nope, I'm going to stand back and watch the show."

Parking Jodi's crazy, I stalked back along the corridor toward the private room where Taylor would be in conference with his favored advisors and Martin Zander. Pulling the gun from the holster, I checked it over before slotting it back.

No one stopped me when I pushed the door open and entered the room. A jolly fucking scene with Taylor relaxing before the big windows that offered views over the river.

I had a vague notion that my rapid entry caused a few raised brows from both the political worms and the four heavily armed guards on duty within, but I didn't let that deter me. I walked straight up to Martin Zander, drew my gun, and put a bullet in his head.

Blood splattered over the table and those too close to the action.

Gasps, cries, and even a scream—I thought that might have been Harris—greeted this development, and every gun in the room trained on me.

"Everyone, calm down," Taylor said, rising from his seat and holding both hands out and up to settle the occupants before directing a glare my way. "What the fuck, Blaine?"

Zander hadn't arrived alone, and the sound of the weaselly ass who'd accompanied him hyperventilating filled the smaller conference room.

"Sorry," I said, not feeling remotely sorry. "He needed to die."

I caught a faint twitch of Taylor's lips before he shook his head. "Relax, everyone. If Blaine said he needed to die, he needed to die."

He nudged his head at Zander's hyperventilating friend. "Does he need to die too?"

I shrugged. "No idea."

Taylor chuckled because the crazy bastard was into violence. He put his hand on the shoulder of Zander's sidekick, making the other man flinch. "Looks like my expansion plans have been brought forward."

Yeah, I'd figured something was off when he'd mentioned an alliance. Taylor didn't do alliances. "I've got stuff I need to deal with."

His lips twitched again before his face smoothed out as he inclined his head in approval. I realized then, perhaps for the first time, that I had his complete trust.

Carter

After Blaine left, I was called to Taylor, which in my opinion did not bode well. My brother had just shot and killed the man our king had been standing up with on the stage.

Taylor needed a doctor, I was told, and I didn't have a choice. Despite Blaine's assurance that Taylor wasn't pissed, I didn't want to take Nora into whatever had transpired for them to need an emergency care doctor.

A few scenarios crashed through my mind as we were escorted to a room at the back of the conference center. Martin Zander had brought some of his people here, as was the norm. It seemed likely there would be repercussions after Zander's death.

"What's happening?" Nora whispered to me as the soldiers walked us up to the door. "Is this to do with Ava? Is she going to be okay? Did Blaine really just shoot her uncle?"

"I don't know the details, babe," I said. "It'll be fine. Blaine has got Ava's tracker—he'll bring her back, I promise." *I hope.* "If it's bad, just look away. We'll leave as soon as we can."

I was expecting a blood bath. What I got was Taylor with a woman on his lap. She was screaming and thrashing. Taylor was trying to restrain her.

I froze.

The door behind me opened as I was still reeling from this development, and a soldier handed me a field medical kit.

"Don't just stand there," Taylor grunted. "Give her something before she hurts her damn self!"

I'd been asked to do many things in my time since I had first met Taylor. Sedating a woman was a line I was not prepared to cross.

"Ava?"

It was Nora who broke the shocked impasse, her fingers clutching mine in a death grip.

The woman recoiled at the name, the fight leaving her for the briefest moment during which I caught sight of luminous winter blue eyes before she fell to broken sobbing.

Ava? She wasn't Ava, this woman's hair was blonde where Ava was dark, and her face bore the subtle lines of age. But those eyes, I could have sworn I would never see the like again. Yet here they were, red-rimmed and staring back at me with so much pain.

"Not quite," Taylor said. "Her mother."

Blaine

I had underestimated Ava in just about every way. Despite Carter notifying the guards as soon as he noticed she was missing, she had already hacked her tracker, ditched the cell, and crossed the river, taking her out of Taylor's jurisdiction.

I was impressed.

I was fucking angry.

As if I didn't have enough to deal with, Taylor called me as we were leaving.

Ava's mother wasn't dead. She was alive and had gone into shock after hearing the daughter she thought she'd lost had run out into the lawless outside alone.

Then the bastard threatened to kill me slowly if I didn't bring Ava back safe and well.

I pushed it all down and focused on the task at hand.

The river's far shore was a no man's land where the lawless outsiders vied for the scraps.

Ava had several agreed rendezvous points with Jodi in case of emergency, which Jodi had only disclosed after I'd killed Zander. I'd be dealing with her for that later, although I couldn't find it in me to blame her. I was new to Ava, had known her a few weeks, and the two women had a history that covered years.

I couldn't see Ava reaching any of the rendezvous points, even assuming she had anything with her for GPS.

Taylor didn't poke his nose in when I organized a small team to take boats to the other side. We'd run reconnaissance over there a few times, but not in the last year. It wasn't even on Taylor's expansion plans. Too much scrubby forest, not enough inhabitants, and nothing else resource-wise to interest the king.

What they did have was a few beaten communities run by the kind of thugs who made Taylor look like a saint. It would be a long trek for her to the only bridge to cross back to this side. Unless she tried to swim again, which I did not like the idea of, given the currents.

I still put patrols on the length of the river.

Despite what the old movies would have you believe, tracking a person wasn't easy when they didn't have an electronic tracker turned on. She was on her own, no boat, and unless she had dropped something that didn't get buried in the deep mud lining the far shore, we were likely to be out of luck.

We were out of luck.

Dark came.

Dawn came.

Finally, I got a call from Mitch to say they'd reactivated her hacked tracker.

She had been taken because there was no other way she could have gotten to Havoc without transportation, and no one would go there by choice.

Chapter Twenty-Three

Ava

Deep in the night, when cold and exhaustion had taken their toll, I realized too late that my boot had caught a tripwire.

I ran.

They came with flashlights and dogs.

And although I fought with all my wild desperation, one punch to the stomach and I was retching on the floor.

"Grab her, Karl!"

A dark shape loomed above me: lank, ratty hair, a thick black beard and bald head, and stocky with muscle. As Karl fisted my hair and dragged my still heaving body from the floor, I acknowledged that a man would always be stronger than a woman and that no amount of training could ever make us equal.

"Got ourselves some pretty little fresh meat here, Bill," the toothless thug said, his stinking breath in my face. His sweaty odor washed over me, making me gag again.

Raucous laughter greeted this statement from the crowd of five, maybe six men, who surrounded me. A pair of mastiffs strained against their chain leashes, two hundred pounds of muscle excited by the chase.

"That we do," the man who approached still had his front teeth, clean-shaven, weathered features, made harsh in the flashlight. "Hold the dogs back," Bill said. "Thought it was gonna be one of them biker prospects again. But ain't this a fine treat." He stepped up to me, running a rough finger down my cheek.

"Where'd you think she came from?" the one who's fist was burning my scalp asked. "Soaked through. Think she swam the river?"

"Reckon she ran from Grimm's," a man from the gathered crowd said. "Maybe we should hand her over. Don't want no trouble stirred up with those mean bastards."

"Well, she's on our turf now," Bill said, stepping back. "Plenty of creeks around these parts between us and Grimm. You run from the bikers, girl?"

I shook my head.

Leaning back, he pinched my cheeks, turning my face toward the flashlight. He whistled. "Look at those pretty eyes. Pupils ain't dilated, and they like to keep their girls on that shit." He released me. "They come looking for her, then they'll have to negotiate. Ain't nothing for free. If she's theirs, they'll pay to get her back. If she ain't, they'll pay, too."

Binding my wrists in rough rope, they marched me through the forest, keeping me motivated to move with a push, slap, or by letting the slavering dogs snarl at me.

I walked, knowing I had no choice.

Knowing too that my attempt to flee my uncle had delivered me to something far worse.

Blaine

It took longer than I wanted to pull everything together. Small team or a large team? They both had merits.

A large team would give us plenty of back up, but it would also draw attention.

A small team could cross via the river, which would be less dangerous, but also slower given we'd have to cover the land on foot.

Slower wasn't working for me. Every second Ava was in Havoc was a second she could be getting raped or beaten, or both. In the end, I decided to go in heavy.

Havoc wasn't the only danger on that side of the river. Grimm's Law was a biker gang we'd been watching for a while. They liked to cross over from time to time. The ever-expanding borders to Taylor's controlled lands were getting harder to maintain. Guns, drugs, and other valuable commodities, including the human variety, were frequently smuggled in and out. They had chapters in several of the outlying areas, and we would need to skirt their main base to reach Havoc.

And again, to get back out.

Jodi wanted in on the operation.

I didn't want to take her. She was an unknown, and while I thought I could trust her, I wasn't a hundred percent. Giving the crazy bitch a weapon was a complication I could do without.

In the end, it was Jodi who convinced me of her inclusion. "You killed him for her," she said. "That's more than I could do. I'm not going to fuck up the operation. But I've been looking out for her long before you stumbled into the picture, and I'm begging you, don't force me to sit this one out."

I nodded and slapped a gun in her hand. "Don't make me fucking regret this."

Ditching the Humvee, we loaded up into lighter, faster armored vehicles. Mitch took the driver seat and Jodi in the back. Another dozen men distributed between us in two more armored vehicles, and we rolled out.

Ava

The magnitude of my impending doom manifested with every exhausting step. The trees opened up into a muddy compound where barking dogs loped the length of mesh fencing as search-lights turned our way.

As the lights panned around us, dirty beatdown structures rose out of the glare into view. A large industrial shed with the big roller doors open, a sprawling farmhouse, a couple of smaller sheds, and a dozen or so trailers.

An old diesel generator growled to the left, thick twisted rope cables leading from it to the buildings and trailers on the right.

The mesh runner gate drew open to allow us entry before it closed on us with an ominous rattle.

A few trailer doors opened, and heads poked out. Some residents hustled back inside, but a few shuffled out into the compound or leaned against doorways as I was escorted through.

A creaking, weathered sign over the farmhouse bore the words 'Welcome to Havoc' in cheery, red paint.

"Get a message to Mick Grimm," Bill called to a scruffy teenage kid emerging from the farmhouse. "Tell him I've got a trade worth a tank of diesel."

The kid lifted a hand before darting back in.

"Where you wanna put her, Bill?"

"Basement," Bill replied. "Make sure the lock's secure and bring me the key. Don't want any of the bitches sniffing around her until Grimm looks her over."

As I was escorted to the farmhouse, I took in the high fencing with coiled barbed wire, the dogs, and the armed men on watch.

I didn't know who this Mick Grimm was, but I had a bad feeling he might have something to do with the biker gang, Grimm's Law.

I began to shake. Karl, my jailor, didn't notice or just didn't care, directing me up the farmhouse's rickety wooden steps. Inside, it stank of weed and sweat. Rough faces peered at me from where they lounged on low, threadbare couches before I was taken left into a filth-strewn farmhouse kitchen with enough greasy, burnt dishes and pans in the sink that I thought no one must have bothered washing since the apocalypse came through. Karl shoved me down narrow wooden steps leading off the kitchen opposite the window. At the bottom, he opened a heavy metal door before sending me sprawling inside. Dusty boxes, hemp sacks, and shelving filled with tins were all I saw before the door slammed shut, sealing me into darkness.

Failing a miracle, I wasn't getting out of here.

Chapter Twenty-Four

Blaine

Taylor owned the bridge and a barren stretch of land where it crossed, and that was it. The razed section gave way to a scrubby forest, and a rutted tarmac road meandered south through the trees that hadn't been serviced since the collapse. Most of the smaller communities that had once thrived here had been looted and turned to ghost towns.

Our convoy blasted through main streets where decaying shops and homes had fallen prey to both weather and encroaching weeds. We slipped from the only main road before reaching the turn for Grimm's territory, taking a five-mile detour through a warren of dirt tracks.

It remained quiet, and even if anyone spotted us, chances were they wouldn't know where we were headed or why.

I'd sent a couple of snipers on bikes ahead of us to reconnoiter Havoc, and I'd just gotten a message that Grimm's Law were on site—a complication we didn't need.

"Does this change the plan?" Mitch asked.

I tapped my communicator bud. "Do they still have chain link fencing?"

"*Chain link fencing around the perimeter. Roller chain link gate,*" came the reply.

"Current site status?"

"*Five guards are walking the perimeter, all are looking twitchy. Two of Grimm's men are at the farmhouse door. We've counted eight bikes—the rest of his crew must be inside.*"

"ETA three minutes," Mitch said like I didn't already know.

"We're coming in hot. Take any and all targets."

The confirmation came through the communicator.

"We going to pop the gate?" Mitch asked, side-eyeing me as I slipped my helmet on.

"Yep, gun it. What's the worst that happens?"

Ava

It was hard to judge how much time had passed, but I thought it several hours later when the basement door was flung open. My jailor, Karl, collected me and dragged me up the stairs.

Thirsty and disorientated, my hands were still bound together and my fingers going numb. I stumbled several times before he thrust me into the farmhouse kitchen.

Blinking against the sudden light, I found a dozen rough-looking men crowding the room, evenly split between the rednecks who had captured me and bikers.

Other than Bill and Karl, I recognized no one. All were armed with guns and knives.

My mouth turned to dust, and my ears filled with white noise.

The nearest biker stalked up to me. I backed up into Karl, my breath turning choppy as the man pinched my chin painfully between his fingers when I stopped breathing altogether.

As he swiped the hair back from my brand, his eyes narrowed and he thrust away.

"Are you fucking stupid?" He rounded on Bill. "Fucking hicks. Did you check her fucking brand?" He got right up into Bill's face.

"Mick, I swear I don't know what you're talking about?" Bill said.

Collective feet shuffled, creaking the scuffed floorboards as hands twitched toward weapons.

"You're too fucking stupid to live," Mick said. "Should've tossed her in the river. That's Taylor's branding, elite forces to be precise." He punched the smaller man with the side of his fist. "What do you think's going to happen now, hick?" He hit Bill again.

"The fuck, man," someone muttered.

"I don't know," Bill said, eyes darting from me to Mick.

"Did you even scan her for a tracker?"

Bill shook his head.

A cry came from beyond the window, followed by the distinct sound of automatic weapons.

All heads swung toward the window.

"Fucking stupid hick," Mick growled.

Bill made a harsh gurgling sound, and my eyes honed in on the knife buried in his chest.

A great crash came from outside, screeching metal on metal, and the roar of an engine. The frozen occupants of the room surged to draw weapons and take cover.

Despite Mick's determination that I might be tracked, I knew I couldn't be. This moment was my one and only opportunity. Smaller and weaker I may be, but I was also fast and fierce, and had learned the importance of committing when it came to close fighting.

My bound fists swung for Karl. I moved my body with them, lending force to the blow.

He doubled over. My knee came up and my forearms came down.

I would never be a man's equal. If they got a good hold on me, or worse punched me, it was over.

Disarm or disable and run like hell, Jodi had drummed into me.

Karl was surprised enough to release me. That was all I needed.

A man was on the back door, everyone else was at the windows, weapons trained.

The route to the lounge was open so that was where I ran.

Blaine

Our armored vehicle plowed through the front gates, ripping them clean off the runner and sending them crashing into a nearby trailer. The snipers had done good. I counted four bodies lying on the ground; another body bounced off the hood as Mitch drove straight over the corner of the collapsed gate and plowed into the farmhouse porch.

Updates bombarded my communicator as we came to a juddering stop, wood and glass raining over the vehicle's nose.

"Hold!"

Bullets sprayed my door before ceasing abruptly.

"You're clear."

We dropped out the side, returning fire. I could see Ava's dot on my visor display. She was in the house, moving toward us, then running away.

Twenty feet separated us.

I gave the signal to Mitch and Jodi that I was going in.

Mitch slammed his back to the left of the busted-up door, Jodi took the right.

I gave the countdown... Three... two... one.

Kicking the door down, I stormed inside, Mitch and Jodi right behind me.

We took the room like the new apocalypse had arrived. Precise, deadly, making every shot count.

Blood sprayed, and dying men screamed.

Then I saw her, hands tied, and the thick-necked biker thug with his hand around her waist. No clean shot—I ran full tilt toward her. Their tussling slammed them up against a table. My little wildcat grabbed a thick, metal-based monstrosity of a lamp and slammed it in his face.

Good girl.

He released her, and my bullet went straight through his chest.

She screamed when I plowed into her, taking her down to the floor and putting my body between her and the firefight in the room. I ripped my helmet off when she continued to thrash and fight. "It's me, baby. Are you hurt?" Her small bony fists connected with my ear.

"Fuck! Ava, it's me!"

The fight left her as quickly as it arrived. Around us, the room fell quiet other than our hard breathing, the occasional groan, and the heavy tread of boots as the team moved around.

"We're clear in here," Mitch called. "Team's mopping up outside, so sit tight for a while."

I rocked back onto my hands and knees so I could see her. "Are you hurt anywhere?" Her cheek was all banged up where some asshole had taken a swipe. Taking my knife out, I cut through the binding on her wrists, ready to pound the shit out of the dead bodies when I saw the split, bruised skin. Her sobs as the blood rushed back filled my gut with rage and ice. "I know, baby, let me see. Wriggle your fingers for me."

Her clothes were still on, and I hated that I even needed to worry about that.

She didn't wriggle her fucking fingers, the little brat. "Move your damn fingers, or your ass is going to pay the price." The scowl she cut my way was pure evil, but weirdly, it settled a notion that she was going to be okay. She finally did as I asked. "Good girl, now make a fist for me."

"It hurts!"

"I know, but hurting is good in this case, and you can make a fist, so that's even better." I turned her face so I could see the shiner on her cheek, running my thumb gently over the swelling. "Any dizziness?"

"No, I just feel bruised everywhere and exhausted. I'm so exhausted."

Footsteps approached, and I knew from Ava's expression who it was going to be.

They were always going to meet at some point. I needed not to act like an asshole about it. Especially now when Ava was hurting after her ordeal.

Steeling myself, I got to my feet and helped Ava up. My eyes played ball between them as I relinquished Ava's hand. There was a world of emotion between the two women. A guttural sob from Ava. A deep groan and devastation on Jodi's face as she wrapped the smaller woman in her arms.

I felt like an intruder.

I wanted to rip Jodi away.

Instead, I snatched up my helmet from the floor, pulled the ear communicator out, and tucked it in my ear.

The compound was dealt with, but we had an angry horde of Grimm's Law incoming and their leader who had been sighted here, was missing.

It wasn't over yet. Time to head home.

Ava

Jodi was holding me so tight, I could feel my ribs creak—a steady, comforting presence that had been part of my life for many years. The how or why she was here with Blaine and that they had found me didn't matter. In this precious interlude, I had everything I needed.

"Tell me you're really okay with him, Ava," she whispered in my ear.

"I'm really okay," I said.

"Good," she said, and I could hear the amusement in her voice. "Because I think I like the asshole, and I'd hate to have to kill him."

I snorted out a tired laugh. It felt so good to laugh.

"We need to leave." Blaine's gruff voice roused me. I lifted my head.

The slightest tightening of Jodi's arms preceded her releasing me. "Stay strong," she said to me. "Things are about to get much better." Then to Blaine, she said, "I'll take point with Mitch." Her lips tugged up in a wicked smirk that told me anyone getting in our way was about to get fucked-up.

When I looked at Blaine, I saw the questions on his face... and fear. There was no hesitation when I went to him, cupped his face, and pulled him down so that his lips could meet mine.

Heaven right here, right now.

A distant sound of automatic fire and the moment was over. His head swung in the direction of the door, and a veil lowered over his face. The flashback of him storming into the room, taking down the threats, brought a full body shiver.

At the time, I hadn't realized it was him—now I did.

Chapter Twenty-Five

Ava

I could hear the roar of approaching bikes as we climbed over the shattered wood and the busted door. An SUV had mounted the farmhouse porch steps and taken out a support pole for the porch roof, which had partially collapsed over the vehicle. Jodi ran across the compound yard, calling to another man as Blaine directed me into the vehicle.

My hands shook so badly, it took me three attempts to get the seatbelt clip into the slot. By the time I was done, Blaine had shoved the vehicle into reverse, bounced down the busted steps, and was speeding out of the compound.

Roaring bikes flashed past the window, and bullets tore into the driver's side in a series of dull pops that set my frayed nerves on edge. "It's bulletproof," he said. "They won't get through."

It didn't make me feel a whole lot better.

Darkness swallowed us as we bounced over ruts so deep they nearly flung me from the seat. Blaine's face was tight and voice terse as he issued commands through the communicator hooked around his right ear. The bikes were gaining on us again, deep, growly engines bringing the promise of revenge.

An explosion rocked the vehicle, and I glanced over my shoulder to see a bike go spinning in the air.

Another explosion, and another.

"We're clear," Blaine said. "You okay?" His focus was on the rutted tarmac road, but he cut a glance in my direction when I didn't answer. We were driving at such a terrifying speed that my eyes had trouble keeping pace, and my stomach felt like I was perpetually tumbling.

"Yes, I think so." That was a lie. I was sure I would never be okay again. Since leaving Guilder City yesterday I'd existed on an adrenaline high of terror. My system was now so wound up it would probably take a week to bring me down.

"That's good because I am going to beat your fucking ass so hard, you won't sit for a week when I get you home."

My heart gave an alarming blip, pushing me straight back to that heightened state of awareness, only this time it wasn't only fear.

The reason I'd fled came crashing back.

"I can't go back," I said, my voice quiet against the steady thrum of the engine.

"You'll go wherever the fuck I say."

I shouldn't have been surprised by this statement. Everything he'd done and said since the day he picked me up from that rooftop had made it clear he would never let me go. I should be horrified by his highhandedness. Instead, it comforted me and made me sad that my reasons for leaving remained valid.

I cared about him—I could admit that it was love. It would destroy me if he were hurt trying to protect me from Martin.

The stomach-churning cries that had filled the farmhouse

were still fresh in my mind. The world held good people, bad people, and everything between. Then the collapse came in like an amplifier it exaggerated their personality traits to the extreme. The men who'd taken me as a prisoner were the bad kind and their last moments had been brutal.

I swallowed against the rising sickness in the pit of my stomach. Blaine could be a stone-cold killer, merciless for those who got in his way, but he had a moral compass of sorts. He was also insanely possessive, and I believed him when he said he'd never let me go.

"Good job we managed to hack back into your hacked tracker," he said.

So that was how they found me.

A dead space opened up in my chest, a sense of desolation that he wasn't going to let me go and that I would be forced to watch him die.

He wasn't like Jodi. Jodi could do some foolish things, but she would never go after Martin. Blaine would absolutely go after him.

I couldn't go back, even after all of this.

"I didn't ask you to save me," I said, voice brittle.

His fist slammed into the dashboard. The sudden violence of the action and the dull smack of the impact ripped a short scream from my lips. My abused nerves sent a rapid shot of adrenaline careening through my body that coiled me up like a spring and then cut me as loose as a noodle when my brain recognized the lack of genuine threat.

He made a pinching motion with the thumb and finger of one hand. "Ava, I'm this close to losing it. You think I don't know what your little stunt was about? You think I can't handle that bastard you call an uncle?" He shook his head. "You don't know me very well."

He was right; I didn't know him very well. All we did was

fall on one another like a pair of horny teenagers. We were both well past that age and well past those excuses. The man sharing the car with me was a stranger, wild, and capable of great violence. I'd never seen anyone kill that efficiently before. The way he'd taken down the men in the room was cold and precise. Perhaps he could handle Martin? Maybe I should have let him in?

My mind began scrambling to work out why Jodi hadn't mentioned Martin. Did she know Martin was schmoozing up with Taylor? I'd been caught up in happy land just after they stormed the farmhouse, but now everything came crashing back. "It isn't your problem," I said quietly.

Blaine's laugh was humorless. "Not my problem? I own you, in case you've forgotten, which makes everything you do my fucking problem until I say otherwise or one of us is dead."

Despite everything that had happened, the thought of him passing me off still hurt worse than anything I'd endured. When I fell, I went all in. "You go after Martin, and you'll be the one who's dead. I can't let you do that." I felt cold and sick as I realized he was going to do precisely that.

"Your faith in me is truly amazing," he growled.

"You don't know him like I do." Anything to do with Martin tied my stomach in knots. The things he'd done... such pain would never go away. I couldn't be at his mercy again. I couldn't endure that. "He killed my father," I whispered. "Then he abused, tormented, and killed my mother."

A sob erupted from my chest. Not once had I told anyone. Jodi was the only person who knew. The raw edge of my emotions, even after all this time, unhinged my self-control. I wanted out of the car, and I fumbled at the seatbelt release before I'd worked out what I'd do after.

"Hey!" Fingers bit into the bones of my wrist, and tears

pooled in my eyes. But a mad need for freedom consumed me, and I fought wildly.

The pressure only increased until I was sure my bones were about to snap.

"He's dead," Blaine said. "I killed him."

I couldn't see past the dull, agonizing ache in my wrist. He retained a hold, but the pressure was no longer absolute.

"He's dead?" My voice came from a long way away, and my ears started to ring.

"Yes, he's dead. Damn it!" His fingers crushing my wrist again snapped me back from the edge. "I can't stop, Ava. Keep it together, baby."

I started to shake; it seemed to well up from deep within until it consumed my whole body. The events at the farmhouse battered at my mind: the sickening shrieks, the hideous cracks of bones breaking, of things being ripped and torn, the barrage of tiny explosions as each bullet was released were like a thousand hammers in my head. Blood... there had been so much blood.

Was my uncle really gone?

"Hey!" My eyes found his briefly before his attention returned to the road. "It's over now," he said softly.

The debilitating tension eased a notch, enough for me to draw deep, steadying breaths into my lungs.

"I need to put my hand back on the wheel," he said.

I nodded.

"You're in shock, baby."

His acknowledgment of my reactions as normal further aided to bring calm. His fingers squeezed over mine gently before he returned them to the wheel.

"I'm not sure how to say this, but your mother's not dead. I'm not sure why you thought she was, but she came with Zander."

I shook my head. "No. That's not possible." I felt a crazy urge to climb out of the car again. "Don't do this to me. Don't—I just can't. I can't relive the grief over again. He killed her. Martin killed her."

The tumbling words stopped.

"Jodi spoke to her," he said. "She seemed certain about who it was."

My mind went looping and looping and not settling anywhere until there was nowhere to go but the burgeoning possibility that my mother was indeed alive. Jodi wouldn't lie about this.

I allowed myself to explore the possibility that it was true, and that Martin had simply lied to me like he'd done so many other times. Why had he done it? To punish me? To show me his power over my life and my mother's? His reasons were incomprehensible.

Were it not so serious, I might have laughed that his deception was the one thing that gave me the courage to leave. I'd never have gone had I known she lived—would never have left her alone with that monster.

Guilt washed over me because I *had* abandoned my mother. What had Martin told her? Had he laughed and cruelly informed her that I'd run away thinking she was dead, or worse, that I'd deserted her?

And then I'd run again. "How is she? Does she know about me?"

"She had to be sedated," he said. "But otherwise, she's fine physically at least. She believed you were dead; finding out you were alive and had fled to the lawless outside didn't go down so well. Carter is taking good care of her. But, baby, it would've crushed her if I hadn't gotten to you."

My mind flittered without purpose from one troubling thought to the next in a kaleidoscope of emotions before settling on the wondrous news—*My mother is alive, and I'm going to see her again.*

"I need you to trust in me, Ava," he said. "To trust that I can protect you. Can you do that?"

Could I?

"I—how did he die?" A macabre thought, but one that needed to be addressed before I could fully move on. A sick inner voice demanded I ask to see the body—no, I wasn't going there.

I watched his profile, saw the moment his lips tugged up before he glanced across at me. "I walked into the room where he was having a meeting with Taylor and their respective advisors and shot him in the head. That work for you, baby? I promise, no one's going to reanimate him with a three inch hole in his skull and half his brains splattered over the wall."

"Jesus!"

His smile dropped. "Tell me you fucking trust me. Tell me you'll fucking talk to me before you do something like this again, or I swear to God, you're never leaving that apartment again, and I'm locking every bit of tech away."

The determination I'd had back on that desolate rooftop as Sanctuary fell came back full force. "I trust you. I won't do it again."

His hand left the steering wheel and closed over mine. A simple touch that spoke of many things. But mostly that from here on, I could and should trust him.

Ownership.

How I'd hated that word and all it represented. Belonging to someone went against every law we'd fought so hard for in the world before the collapse. But here, in the after, it was neither cloying nor repelling.

It felt just right.

The tall skyscraper Blaine took me to made the one we lived in look drab. My mother was in here, I was told. Blaine, rightly determining that I wasn't going to be happy until I'd seen her, brought me to her.

"There's a lot of empty floors," Blaine said by way of explanation as we ascended toward the penthouse floor in the elevator. He had his arm looped around my waist, chin resting on the top of my head. I felt the same level of need to touch. I'd damaged things by not trusting him, and it would take time for that to heal.

"I don't understand why she's with Taylor," I said. "Is she a prisoner?"

"Me neither," Blaine said. "But he doesn't see personally to the care of prisoners, so I'd say don't worry, except Taylor's a power-hungry psycho." He glanced up at the corner of the elevator where a camera sat. "So who knows."

I rationalized he was teasing me. I *hoped* he was teasing me.

Nerves exploded as the door opened onto a plush lobby. A tall, built man, who was obviously security, showed us through to a lounge. I barely took in the stunning decadence of the palatial setting or Carter, who sat on the periphery with an elderly woman. My focus was all on the woman I'd thought I'd lost forever.

A sob caught in my throat as I saw the hope and joy I felt mirrored on her face. Fragile, haunting in her beauty—god, I had missed her. I froze under the weight of the emotional avalanche before rushing to her. We both tried to speak, a disjointed babble that didn't make a bit of sense.

The words didn't matter. The connection did.

We cried, we laughed, and we clung to each other.

Time passed. Distantly, I was aware of Carter leaving and of Blaine talking to Taylor.

"I thought you were dead," I said when I could finally get the words out. I couldn't bring myself to use my uncle's name, nor even to think of him as a relative. "*He* told me you were dead."

Her hand cupped my cheek. "I don't know why he would do that, Alexis. I've spent too many years with him, and I don't understand half the things he did and said. He liked to make threats. He was a bully and a monster." Her eyes searched mine. "When he told me you'd gone, I'd never felt such relief. I hoped you were in a better place. I'm so relieved Jodi was with you."

"I'm so sorry I left you." Fresh tears streamed down my cheeks.

"Don't be. Never be sorry for that." She smiled through the tears. "How could you know that he hadn't killed me as he'd said? And after what he did to Gregory?" Her lips trembled at the mention of my father's name, and she drew a ragged breath. "That's the first time I've felt safe to speak his name for many years."

I pressed my forehead to her's clinging once again. "We'll use his name from now on," I said. "As often as we want."

"It's going to take time," she said. "I've got a lot of grieving to do. But already, I feel like I can breathe."

We talked more until exhaustion won out, and still hugging each other on the couch, I fell into a light doze.

"You need to get some rest, Alexis," my mother said. Easing back, she inspected me with the critical eye all mothers have.

I nodded. "You must come back home with us. We can talk more tomorrow."

"She stays here." The voice that spoke carried authority. I looked up to find Taylor watching us—watching my mother. "I have a doctor here," he indicated the elderly woman with steel grey hair who had been talking to Carter when I arrived. "And your mother has been through several significant shocks." Yeah, that was down to me. Dark eyes held mine—the man certainly had a formidable presence.

I went to protest, but both my mother and Blaine waded in.

"You can see her tomorrow," Blaine said. "I think your capacity for making demands isn't great, given I've just started a war with Grimm's Law to get you back."

My mother's sharp hiss saw Blaine catch a glare from Taylor. The king seemed protective toward my mother... and there was a doctor here.

My mother squeezed my hand. "I've gotten to be a good judge of a person's character over the years. I promise this will be fine."

I went home with Blaine. "So," he said as I hopped up beside him in the Humvee. "Your real name is Alexis?"

I smiled. "Just Ava now."

He smiled back. "Fine, just Ava, let's head the fuck back home."

For once, we didn't fall on one another, and with the comforting weight of his arms around me, I fell into a deep sleep.

True to my mother's word, she was fine, and the next day, we began the long journey toward healing the horrors of our past.

Chapter Twenty-Six

Nora

Life had barely settled again after the drama surrounding Ava's flight and the subsequent reunion with her mother when my life was once more thrown into the spin by a proposition for ownership.

He didn't look like a thug this time, but the man was obviously a soldier, and I greeted the request for my owner's name with all the composure of a deer caught in headlights. I mumbled Carter's name and went and hid in the bathroom for ten minutes. Deep breaths, and I hit call... it went straight to voicemail. My throat was so tight, not a single word came out.

I ended the call and tried to send him a message. My hands were shaking so badly, the letters turned to gibberish.

I was splashing water over my face to try and find calm when a nurse entered. Carol was a sweet older lady and nothing like Gilly. The latter had found herself reallocated to the field hospital operations permanently—or so I'd heard.

Word was, Carter was behind this. I thought I ought to feel sorry for field hospital operations, but I really didn't.

"What's happened?" Carol asked, placing her hand on my shoulder. "You're as white as a sheet."

"I need to message Carter," I said. "A man—"

I couldn't even bring myself to speak it.

Her face softened. "Want me to call him for you?"

"Voicemail," I said. Strangely, I felt calmer now that Carol was here. "I'm going to send him a message. It just shocked me."

"Of course," she said kindly. "I know Gilly set you up last time. I've heard she's gone to a new owner—he's not as soft as the last one." Her lips set in a disapproving line. "About time if you ask me... Best to get the message done sooner rather than later. And don't leave the building before he acknowledges it."

I nodded. My fingers only shook a little this time, and I tapped the message out.

The reply came back instantly.

Carter: *I'll deal with it.*

Carter

I had an office at the medical center adjoining the research labs. Although I'd spent more than average time dealing with the influx of emergencies over the last few weeks, I'd been given leave to return to my genetics research today. I was still very much a junior doctor, despite being fast-tracked through the basics.

It made a nice change to get back to work that didn't involve partially severed limbs and shrapnel damage. I'd

Owned

become hardened to such horrors long before arriving at Guilder City—you did what you could.

I spent the morning in the lab before heading to a small adjoining ward where we administered the genetic enhancements. My cell rang as I dealt with a soldier who'd had a severe reaction to the viral enhancement. It didn't happen very often, but it was a known risk, and it took us a short while to stabilize him.

Once this was done, I glanced down at my cell to find a message from Nora.

A volatile mix of emotions assaulted me as I read it. Relief that Nora had trusted in me and messaged me as I'd asked. White-hot fury that some asshole dared to set his sights on what was mine. But also that human fear of fallibility.

I shot off a quick reply.

Nora was relying on me. There wasn't room for doubts in this scenario—I needed to send a message to the asshole who dared to challenge for Nora.

I found ward staff not very subtly loitering when I arrived on the floor.

Nosey bastards. Not that I could blame them. I remembered a time before I claimed ownership when such escapades were viewed with curiosity.

I gave them a stern glare as I passed the nurse's station, which sent a few of them scurrying to whatever they were supposed to be doing. A few toughed it out and blatantly watched me pass.

When I reached the cubical in question, I stepped inside and yanked the curtain across.

"She's not available," I said, folding my arms and eyeballing

203

my competition, who was disadvantaged by being on a bed and recently injured. As Blaine would say, go hard and go early.

...mid-thirties, a soldier, and solid muscle from what I could tell. He gave me the kind of look I got all the time, the one that said I was a barely credible doctor, and certainly nothing to deter him from a challenge.

"You're a doctor, right?" he said, fronting relaxed by placing a hand behind his head. "If she's not pregnant by your pencil dick, then she's available. I heard you won a challenge a while ago. Someone must have helped you."

I'd flipped the handy velcro strap over one wrist and pinned the other to the bed before he could let out more than a squeak.

"The fuck are you doing, asshole?" he said, but there was a nervous tremble in his voice that I enjoyed.

"There's a scalpel against your throat. You probably won't even feel it slide in."

"Get the fuck off of me!"

"Yes, that wet trickle is blood. It'll start to sting soon." He went deathly still. "No one helped me in the challenge. Unless you're referring to my brother turning up and making sure it stayed one-on-one—my challenger brought ten of his buddies and a corrupt adjudicator. Are you the kind of man who challenges off the grid? Because if you are, I'm just going to slit your throat and save Blaine the trouble of tossing your ass outside, like he did with the last low-life."

"I'm not into underhand challenges, man."

"Glad to hear it." I stepped back, dropping the bloody scalpel on the nearby cart. "They had to scrape my last challenger off the underground garage floor. I'm sure the footage is still doing the rounds if you want to check." I flipped the velcro on his other wrist, and his only move was to press his fingers to his throat and check for blood.

My smile was cold. "Stay the fuck away from Nora or issue the challenge."

He raised both hands. "I'm good."

When I turned and wrenched open the curtain, half a dozen ward staff nearly fell in. "Tell Nora I'll see her in my office," I said before stalking away.

Nora

I went and hid in the stock room when I heard via the medical center grapevine that Carter was on his way to the ward. I didn't want him to get hurt again. I felt stupid and foolish that anyone was even making these sorts of requests.

My head was deep in the proverbial sand, but it was dark and safe with your head down and ass up.

I wallowed in this state of denial until my cell bleeped with a message from Carter asking me to report immediately to his office. Stomach in knots, and fearing I would be forced to watch him fight the man, I dragged my feet all the way, wallowing in denial, and praying for fate to intervene and save us from this nightmare. I arrived before I was mentally ready. The door was closed, forcing me to knock.

"Come in."

The muffled sound of his voice brought a kick to my pulse, and bracing myself, I opened the door.

"Lock the door, and come over here." That stern doctor voice and stoic expression and my heart lodged in my throat.

"Do not fucking test me," he said, but his lips tugged up, and it stilled a little of my franticness. Then I remembered how he'd told me everything would be alright when the drug dealer first challenged and before Blaine arrived. Maybe the challenge was already set.

"Like a fucking animal," Blaine had said afterward. Carter looked so civilized as he sat behind a desk with his crisp white shirt. But I only had to consider how the material was stretched over muscle and the savagery with which he'd eliminated the last threat to understand that where Carter was concerned, first impressions were deceiving.

I didn't want him to fight, but I believed in my very soul that Carter would prevail if he did.

"Babe, I'm still waiting." I think I might have climaxed a little, damn his stern doctor voice. The lock was thrust shut with more force than was necessary. I caught a raised brow as I stomped over and rounded the desk to his side.

Leaning back in his chair, he smirked before shackling a wrist and pulling me onto his lap.

I squealed. He chuckled, and catching hold of my chin, turned my face toward his. "Nora, stop looking so worried. I said I would deal with it. I've dealt with it."

"Already?" My eyes searched his face. He didn't look hurt. "That was—um—fast?"

"We had a talk," he said. "He decided not to pursue the matter."

With those words, all the tension left my body.

"Thank you for trusting me. Thank you for telling me and not hiding from this." His lips tugged up in a smirk. "I admit to having some doubts about how you'd react if it happened again. It's not easy to trust. I get that."

I'd loved Glenn dearly, but he hadn't been a strong man, not physically and not mentally. The many years we'd been on the run, I'd been the one fighting to keep us together and alive. He didn't have a single survival instinct in his body or mind. But surprisingly, the floppy-hair doctor, did.

Owned

He was determined to keep me safe, and I craved a partner who could make some of the life decisions for me so I didn't need to be strong every second of every day.

I was owned. But it was the freest I'd ever been.

His hand cupping my cheek lowered to my throat, his eyes darkened, and I felt his cock thud against my hip. That quickly, I felt my body respond. The fear experienced living every day in this world, of whatever challenge tomorrow might bring manifested a sharp, visceral need for connection in the most basic way.

These interludes between the pain were to be cherished because who knew when it might be snatched away.

"I don't think I have gentle in me," he said, eyes locked with me. "Not after another man challenged me for you."

He was warning me. Giving me an option to walk away and stop this now.

I knew he was going to fuck me roughly, and I welcomed it. Leaning forward, I pressed my lips to his. He groaned softly, nipping at my lower lip before lifting his head. Without a word, he coaxed me up from his lap and bent me over his desk. My hands shook with impatience, pussy already weeping as he tugged my skirt up, panties down, and filled me in a single thrust. "God, yes. That feels so good!"

Every rough stroke seemed to imprint his caring upon me.

"Babe, I told you I'd take care of you. If I have to do this every fucking day so you don't forget, that's what I'm going to do."

"Please, I want you to." The feeling of him moving inside me, the rough thrusts, the strong hands holding me still and forcing me to take this, made me feel gloriously alive.

"You want me to come inside you?"

"Yes, please, yes."

"Do you have any idea what it will do to me if someone

takes you and Adam from me now? The thought of you with some asshole, someone else having this perfect fucking pussy, putting *their* kid in what's mine, makes me see fucking red."

I begged him to come. I pushed back to take every thrust, doing and saying anything in the hope that it might encourage him to come inside me.

I didn't want to climax before him, but the mere desire for abstinence brought it rushing to the fore. The roar as he pounded deeper twisted the sensations up into a wild, gluttonous bounty. Heat washed over my body; I shivered. My pussy clenched over and over.

The release took all my tension. My entire being focused on the hot flesh filling me and making me whole, the fierce, protective body bracing mine over the desk, and our gusty breaths as we both came down.

I could feel the cum leaking, feel his cock jerking as more spilled out.

It was messy.

It was perfect.

I felt complete.

But nothing was forever, and as he left me, I missed the connection.

"Fuck," he muttered, and there was a whole world of meaning in that single word.

I giggled.

It got me a playful smack on the ass. He slumped onto the chair, dragging me onto his lap. I fidgeted. My pussy kept fluttering in little echoes that ached as much as they felt good.

"You sore, babe?"

I nodded. The words stirred at latent emotions bringing the hot tears pooling at the back of my eyes. Not trusting myself to speak without blubbering words of love all over him.

He took my chin, forcing me to meet his eyes. "Good. I

want you to ache where my cock has been. I want you to feel my cum leaking out all day. And I want your pussy all sore deep inside where I've fucked you good and hard. I love you, Nora. You're mine now. I've claimed both you and Adam, put my mark on you."

The shock of what had happened in the last challenge was still fresh, and the tears spilled over my cheeks. "I love you too. I like feeling the way I do after you've been inside me. I think... I think I might need this regularly. To remind me."

His lips tugged up before he leaned in to take my lips in a sweet kiss that set me squirming again.

Epilogue

Blaine

"It's supposed to be a practice!" I called as I passed the gym mat where Jodi and Mitch were having at one another.

"I'm going easy on him, and he's still losing," Jodi said, panting as she took Mitch to the mat in a perfect drop and pinned him there.

"Bitch, we both know *I'm* going easy on you." Mitch grunted as she gave his arm a twist—Jodi added insult to injury by landing a sound spank on his ass.

"The fuck did you just do?" Mitch growled.

I bit back a smirk and carried on just as he broke the hold. They were both bruised and bloody, but something told me they were far from finished yet.

Stowing my practice kit, I grabbed a quick shower before hopping in the Humvee and heading back to Taylor's headquarters, where Ava now worked. Once our illustrious leader had heard about her hacking skills, she'd been allocated to his small Shadow Squad and was happily wreaking havoc.

She'd needed a purpose that didn't involve waiting in my apartment all day for me to come home and screw her brains out.

We still did the latter. Sleep was optional when you had an angel with a magic pussy in your bed. And I was still a territorial prick. I'd told every man and woman in her new team that I would toss them into the lawless outside if they so much as looked at her wrong.

They took me at my word.

The room quieted when I pushed open the door. Computer kits of every imaginable kind filled every available surface. Laptops and computers, whole and empty shells, and everything in between. High bench-tops littered with circuit boards and cables. It looked like chaos to me... according to Ava, this was a form of art.

Ava threw a look over her shoulder, eyes narrowing even as her lips tugged up. Apparently, I was intimidating.

"I'll catch you tomorrow," she said jumping down from the high stool. "Message me if you get it working."

"Don't message her if you get it working," I corrected.

She glared at me as she approached. "Baby," I whispered as she drew level with me. "Thirty seconds after you walk in the apartment door, my dick is going to be buried in your pussy, and the only thing you'll be worried about is when I'm going to let you come."

I saw her little involuntary shiver before she muttered without heat, "You are such a savage."

Swinging the door open, I let her pass through first before cutting a look across the occupants of the room just in case any of them were confused about my order. The door closed shut, and we headed down the corridor toward the exit.

"I—um—asked my mother to come over tonight," she said, face screwing up in a wince when I cursed. "I haven't seen her in days!"

"You saw her two days ago," I said, pushing through the exit door.

"Don't be such a baby," she said, smirking when she saw my glare. "I'll make it up to you."

My mind immediately conjured up an image of her on her knees, lips stretched around my cock. "Yeah?"

"Yes," she agreed. At the Humvee, she stopped and turned to face me instead of getting in. "Thank you." She leaned up on her tiptoes, hands finding the back of my head so she could pull me down for a kiss.

That little peck wasn't going to cut it. I had her ass in my hands and her back against the side of the Humvee with her legs wrapped around my waist so I could seal our deal properly. "What time is she arriving?" I asked when I could drag my lips from hers.

"Seven," she said, eyes glassy, lips swollen, cheeks flushed, and voice a little breathless. If I had my way, she'd spend the rest of her life looking like this.

Checking my watch, I grinned. "Plenty of time to work off some of that debt of gratitude," I said. Dropping her back to the ground, I opened the door and all but threw her in.

One great thing about the post-apocalyptic world... the roads were quiet, and no one cared about what speed you were doing. I tossed her over my shoulder when we parked up at our apartment—she had called me a savage. She squealed and faked outrage the whole way to our apartment door. But once we were closed inside, she looked at me the way I looked at her. Love, hunger, and an unwavering determination that whatever happened next, we were in this together.

About the Author

Thanks for reading *Owned*. Want to read more? Check out the rest of my *Coveted Prey* series and my other books!
Amazon: https://www.amazon.com/author/lvlane

Where to find me...
Website: https://authorlvlane.com
Blog: https://authorlvlane.wixsite.com/controllers/blog
Facebook: https://www.facebook.com/LVLaneAuthor/
Facebook Page: https://www.facebook.com/LVLaneAuthor/
Facebook reader group: https://www.facebook.com/groups/LVLane/
Twitter: https://twitter.com/AuthorLVLane
Goodreads: https://www.goodreads.com/LVLane

Also by L.V. Lane

Prey

I am prey.

This is not pity talking, this is an acknowledgment of a fact.

I am small and weak; I am an Omega. I am a prize that men war over.

For a year I have hidden in the distant corner of the Empire.

But I am running out of food, and I am running out of options.

That I must leave soon is not a decision for today, though, but a decision for tomorrow.

Only tomorrow's choices never come.

For tonight brings strangers who remind me that I am prey.

Prey is a fantasy reverse harem Omegaverse with three stern Alphas, an Alpha wolf-shifter, and a stubborn Omega prey.

Printed in Great Britain
by Amazon

19490691R00128